PARTY GAMES

Also by R. L. Stine

R. L. STINE

PARTY GAMES

A FEAR STREET NOVEL

THOMAS DUNNE BOOKS
ST. MARTIN'S GRIFFIN
NEW YORK

THOMAS DUNNE BOOKS.
An imprint of St. Martin's Press.

www.thomasdunnebooks.com
www.stmartins.com

The Library of Congress Cataloging-in-Publication Data is available upon request.

ISBN 978-1-250-05161-5 (hardcover)
ISBN 978-1-4668-5651-6 (e-book)

St. Martin's Griffin books may be purchased for educational, business, or promotional use. For information on bulk purchases, please contact Macmillan Corporate and Premium Sales Department at 1-800-221-7945, extension 5442, or write specialmarkets@macmillan.com.

First Edition: October 2014

10 9 8 7 6 5 4 3 2 1

To Kat Brzozowski and all my Twitter friends who persuaded me to return to this street of horrors

PARTY GAMES

INTRODUCTION

The Fear Street woods stretch for hundreds of acres at the eastern end of the town of Shadyside. Tall, leafy maple and sycamore trees, centuries old, make the woods shadowy and cool, even on the sunniest days.

The woods are beautiful, fragrant, and quiet. But few Shadyside residents would ever hike or picnic there.

Maybe they know the story of the two girls who were found in the woods—*with all their bones missing.*

Or maybe they know the odd fact that no birds ever venture into these woods or perch on the trees. Most people take that as a *warning.*

Or maybe it's because everyone in town has heard the unexplained, inhuman howls and shrieks that echo off the tall trees late at night.

Everyone in the pleasant, suburban town of Shadyside knows about the Fear family, early settlers of the town, who practiced the black arts and were cursed with a history of untold evil. The woods—and the winding street that bears their name—are places to be avoided by all.

Shadyside High senior Rachel Martin has lived in Shadyside her whole life. She should know better than to venture off with Brendan Fear to an all-night party at his family summer home on Fear Island. She should know there are risks when you get involved with a Fear. But sometimes romance gets in the way of common sense.

Besides, all those scary Fear family stories are ancient history—aren't they?

Aren't they?

Rachel looks forward to a dream weekend. But she is about to learn that Fear Street is where your darkest nightmares live.

—R. L. Stine

PART ONE

1.

THE INVITATION

I saw Brendan Fear walk into the diner where I worked with some of his friends, but I had no idea how my life would change that night. As I wiped down a table, I followed him with my eyes as he led his three friends down the narrow aisle to the booth in the back corner.

How could such a normal scene lead to so much horror—and even murder?

I knew the kids who were with Brendan. I'm not in the same crowd, but we're all seniors at Shadyside High. Ha. *Same crowd.* That's kind of a laugh. Face facts. I have a few good friends, but I definitely don't have a *crowd*.

My name is Rachel Martin, and I'm seventeen. I have this after-school waitress job at Lefty's, a hangout a few blocks from the high school. And yes, it's a teeny-tiny bit awkward to wait on the kids I see in school all day.

But I'm sure that's just me. No one ever makes a

comment or a joke about it. But sometimes it makes me uncomfortable.

I guess I'm not the most relaxed person on the planet. Mom says I'm strung tighter than a tennis racket. My sister, Beth, always insists that's not true. She says I'm just *sensitive.*

I sure miss Beth. She went off to Oberlin in September. Beth got a scholarship for her flute playing. She's the smart one *and* the talented one in the family.

We have always been so close. She said she'd Skype me every night. But I haven't heard from her in weeks.

The kitchen bell rang, the signal that someone's food was ready. I collected some dirty plates from a table and squeezed through the crush of kids at the counter to get to the kitchen.

Lefty's is small and always hot and steamy, no matter what the weather is outside. When I get home after work, I have to shower for a long time to get the fried grease smell of hamburgers and French fries off my skin and out of my hair.

But this place is definitely the most popular hangout for Shadyside High kids, partly because it's so close to school. And because it's The Home of the Two-Dollar Double Cheeseburger.

I don't know who thought that up, but it was genius.

I saw my friend Amy O'Brien walk in. She waved, but I didn't have time to go say hello to her. Ellen, the other waitress, called in sick, and I was covering the whole restaurant.

I carried some cheeseburgers to a table near the front. Then I picked up four menus to take to Brendan Fear's table. He and his friends were all talking at once, leaning toward each other over the table, glancing around as if they didn't want to be overheard. Very intense.

They all stopped talking as I stepped up to them.

I saw Kerry Reacher, who is our All-State forward on the basketball team. He was wearing his maroon-and-white team jacket. He's so lanky, his legs stretched out of the booth. His white sneakers had to be at least size 12 or a 14.

Patti Berger sat next to him. Patti is a sweet-looking dark-haired girl, tiny, like a little doll, with a whispery doll voice and dimples to die for. She's so adorable, you want to kill her. Except she's the nicest person on earth, friendly and warm.

Patti and I grew up together because our moms are best friends. We're not really in the same crowd at school. But we're still happy to see each other whenever our families get together.

Patti is about as tall as a fourth grader. Seriously. I mean, she's got to be two feet shorter than Kerry. But they're always together. They say they're just good friends. But everyone sees them holding hands, lip-locked in the halls. I guess the friends thing is some kind of private joke.

Next to Brendan, Eric Finn was drumming on the tabletop with two fingers. Eric is a big, bouncy teddy bear of a dude, with wavy blond hair, a round freckled face, booming voice, and a loud, hee-haw donkey laugh. He's one of those guys who just likes to laugh and party.

I've always thought it was totally weird that he and Brendan Fear are such good buddies. They're like total opposites. But they've been friends since elementary school.

Brendan has wavy black hair. He is pale and serious-looking. He has this shy smile, but you don't see it very often, and he speaks very quietly. I like his eyes. They're soft brown and warm, kind of crinkly, and when they lock on you, it's like he's seeing into your brain.

Uh-oh. Does that give you a hint that I've had a crush on Brendan Fear since eighth grade?

He dresses in black jeans and black T-shirts with video game logos on the front. He's the school brainiac, but he's totally into games.

He and Eric and some of his other friends play games for hours. *World of Warcraft* and *Grand Theft Auto* and all kinds of fantasy and car-racing games. That's all they talk about at school. And someone told me that Brendan programs his own games and is working with some guys to develop an online gaming site.

I walked up to Brendan's booth with the menus tucked under the arm of my red-and-white-checked uniform.

"Whoa." I tripped over Kerry's big shoes, and stumbled into the table.

Awesome start.

Brendan grabbed my arms and helped stand me up. "Rachel, you okay?" His dark eyes peered into mine.

I could feel my face go hot. I liked the way he said my name.

"I'll move over if you want to sit with us," Eric said. "Or you can sit on my lap?"

Kerry and Patti laughed.

"That would be a thrill," I said. "But would you give me another job when I'm fired?"

He flashed me a devilish grin. "I could think of *something.*"

"Give Rachel a break," Patti told Eric. "Can't you see she's busy?"

"She and I could get busy," Eric said.

Patti gave him a playful slap. "Eric, don't you ever stop joking?"

"Who's joking?"

Eric and I have been teasing each other since first grade. He's always flirting with me, but he flirts with every girl he sees. No one ever takes him seriously because he's never serious.

I handed the menus out to them.

"You work here every day after school?" Brendan asked.

I nodded. "Yeah." I brushed my hair off my forehead

9

with one hand. I could feel sweat on my forehead. I knew I didn't look my best.

"Till when?" Brendan asked. His eyes were studying me.

"Till ten."

"Whoa. Long day. When do you do your homework?"

I shrugged. "Whenever."

"What's homework?" Eric chimed in. "Should I try it?"

"You wouldn't like it," Patti told him.

Brendan kept studying me, like he had something on his mind.

"Waitress? Could we have a check?" A woman at the table behind me tapped my shoulder. It startled me, and I jumped.

"Sure. Just a sec," I said. The door slammed as another bunch of Shadyside kids came in. The diner was getting really crowded.

I turned back to Brendan. "Do you guys know what you want?" I asked.

"Do you have cheeseburgers here?" Eric asked, grinning at me again.

Totally dumb joke.

"No one ever asked for that before," I said. "I'll have to check."

Kerry and Patti laughed. "I'll come back in a few minutes," I said. I glanced back and saw Brendan's eyes following me as I walked away.

I scribbled out the check for Table 4. I had to tear up the first one and start again because I was thinking about Brendan Fear, and my hand was actually trembling a little. Doesn't take much to get me excited.

I mean, those were definitely meaningful looks he was flashing me.

Rachel, he was just trying to make you feel better since you nearly fell into his lap.

Was I imagining the meaningful looks? Face facts. I'm not the most confident person in the world. I think I look okay. I'm not Red Carpet beautiful or anything. I have straight blonde hair, which I usually pull back into a simple ponytail, pale blue eyes, and a nice smile. I think my nose is crooked. And I have sort of a square chin, which I hate. When I'm feeling really low, I think my face looks like an ax blade with eyes.

But Beth says I'm really pretty. She says I look like Reese Witherspoon. She always knows how to cheer me up.

I watched Brendan and his friends talking so intensely. Even Eric had a serious expression on his face. What could they be talking about?

The kitchen bell rang. I hurried to the window to pick up the food. Lefty squinted out at me from the kitchen. His narrow face was bright red and bathed in sweat. He always wears a white baseball cap backward over his bald head.

"You okay, Rachel?"

"Busy night," I said. "But I'm handling it. I—"

Lefty didn't wait to hear my answer. He had turned back to the fry griddle.

I went back to work. So far, I'd made it through with only a few mix-ups.

The diner had emptied out a bit when Brendan and his friends got up to leave. They smiled and nodded to me as they made their way to the door.

"Would you like a tip?" Eric said.

"Sure," I replied.

"Look both ways before crossing the street." He laughed at his own dumb joke.

I was surprised when Brendan stayed back and pulled me aside. Again, he kept his eyes on me as if trying to read my mind.

Maybe he has this intense stare for everyone. He probably doesn't even realize it.

I could feel my chest get a little fluttery. "Was everything okay?" I asked.

He nodded. "Sure." He shifted his weight. He suddenly looked very uncomfortable. "So . . . you work here every night?"

"Not always. It depends on who else can work. Sometimes I'm here on Saturday, too. I need to earn some money to help my family. Things have been kind of tight for them, and I wanted to . . . you know . . . pitch in."

Too much information, Rachel.

He nodded and scratched his dark hair. "You're in my World Government class, right?"

"Yes," I said. "Mrs. Rigby. She's funny. I like her."

"Some guys think she's really hot," he said. He flashed the shy grin.

Someone spilled a Coke at a table near the counter. I heard the glass shatter on the floor. Some kids laughed.

"I wanted to ask you something," Brendan said. He shoved his hands into his jeans pockets. "I'm having this birthday party, see. It's my eighteenth. On Saturday."

"Happy birthday," I said. *Awkward.*

"My family has this huge old summer house on Fear Island. You know. In the middle of the lake? We're opening it up for my party. It's going to be like an overnight thing. We're going to party all night."

The kitchen bell rang. More cheeseburgers to pick up.

Brendan leaned forward. "Think you could come?"

Best day ever?

"*This* Saturday?" I said. My voice came out a little higher than normal.

He nodded. "I'm sending a boat to pick everyone up at the lake dock at the end of Fear Street at two."

"Yes," I said. "I can come. Hey, thanks for inviting me."

"It's going to be an awesome party," he said. "Lots of games."

Lefty banged the bell a few more times.

"I have to get back to work," I said.

Brendan nodded. "See you Saturday." And then he reached out his finger and wiped a drop of sweat off the tip of my nose.

My mouth fell open as he turned and strode to the door.

I could still feel the touch of his finger on my nose. I started to the food window. *Brendan Fear just invited me to his birthday party.*

I stepped up to the counter, but a hand grabbed my wrist and tugged me back.

And a voice whispered in my ear, "Rachel—don't go."

2.

THE WARNING

I turned and tugged my wrist free. "Don't go," Amy O'Brien repeated.

I'd forgotten she was still in the restaurant. Amy is my best friend. We've been friends ever since our sophomore year overnight when we both got lost in the woods and had to be rescued by Mr. Singletary, our homeroom teacher.

Poor guy. I think we gave him a total breakdown that night. He couldn't stop shaking for a week. I guess he thought we were eaten by wolves or something.

Being totally lost at night in the woods is an awesome way to start a friendship. You already know you're both hopeless idiots. Amy and I have been BFFs ever since.

Amy is short and a little chubby, with scads of coppery curls and green cat eyes and creamy skin to die for. She loves the color red and always has a red scarf around her neck or a red top or vest. And she wears this bright red lipstick, called

Wildfire, which her mother says makes her look like a slut. But Amy says red is her trademark.

She squeezed my wrist again. "I heard everything, Rach. Please. Don't go."

"Amy, I have to pick up these plates," I said. I took the food plates off the window counter. I could see Lefty staring at me from the kitchen. I turned and started to carry them to Booth 8.

Amy followed me, pushing her way through a group of men in blue work uniforms waiting for a table. "Rachel, what did you tell him? Did you tell him you'd go?"

I set the plates down and brought the customers ketchup and mustard from the service table behind their booth. I turned to Amy, who was impatiently plucking at the buttons on the front of her red wool jacket.

"Of course I said yes, Amy."

"Shut up. You said yes to a sleepover at Brendan Fear's house?"

"It's not a sleepover. It's a birthday party."

"An *all-night* birthday party, right?"

I sighed. "Amy, I can't talk now. I'm the only one waitressing tonight. I have to help Lefty close up at ten. Want to come over when I'm done?"

"I'll finish my cheeseburger and wait for you. We have to talk. I can't believe you said yes." She walked back to her stool at the counter, shaking her head.

I knew that Amy didn't like Brendan, but I wasn't sure

why. If she had some reason she didn't want me to go to his party, I knew I'd hear about it later. Amy isn't the type to keep her opinions to herself. She's kind of judgmental. But she's smart, and she's usually right.

Only a half hour till closing, but the time seemed to drag on for hours. Finally, everyone had paid up and left. Silence. Except for the sound of Lefty scraping down the grill in the kitchen. I wiped the tables and brought the last of the dirty dishes to the sink. I checked the time on my phone as I stepped out of the diner. It was a little after ten thirty.

It was a cold October night. The frosty air felt good against my hot face. I took some deep breaths, happy to be out of the steamy restaurant. A pale half-moon floated high in the sky above snakes of gray cloud.

Amy waited for me on the corner, her red jacket buttoned to the collar. She had pulled on a red wool cap and wool gloves. She squinted at me. "Wow. You must be tired. You look like roadkill."

"Don't hold back," I said. "Tell me what you really think."

She was right. I was that special kind of tired. The kind where you're so exhausted, even your hair hurts. I had a layer of dried sweat on my skin, and I could smell the fry grease in my hair.

I shifted my backpack on my shoulders. I was supposed to work on two chapters in my science notebook tonight.

But now, forget about it. Amy probably wouldn't go home till midnight.

We crossed Division Street, empty except for a UPS truck making a late stop. It was a short walk to my house, only three blocks away. My legs ached and my back felt stiff. I'd been standing up since four o'clock.

Don't complain, Rachel. You made more than a hundred dollars in tips tonight.

I planned to turn most of it over to my parents. They were having tough times. My dad was laid off last year from his job as director of a big investment company. It took him a long time to find a new job. Now he's working as a shift manager at the Walmart in Waynesbridge.

My mom still hasn't recovered from a really bad case of Lyme disease. She's been home for three months and still feels weak and exhausted all the time.

A strong gust of wind pushed Amy and me back as we started to cross Front Street. Dead leaves danced in a perfect circle around our feet.

"Go ahead," I said. "Let me have it. Give me your lecture about why I shouldn't go to Brendan Fear's party, even though it's going to be awesome."

"Awesome?" She made a snorting sound. "Have you Googled the word *geek*? You can read about Brendan."

"I think he's . . . hot. Seriously."

Amy blinked. "Hot? He's totally weird. He spends all

his time playing video games with that big goofball Eric Finn."

I shook my head. "Amy, you just don't get it. Like, hello—it's the twenty-first century. Geeks rule."

"But, Rachel—"

"Brendan doesn't just play games. He designs his own games, and he does all the programming. He's like a genius. And . . . don't you like the way his eyes crinkle up when he smiles?"

"Forget his eyes," Amy replied, adjusting her hat in the wind. "What are we talking about here? I don't care if you think he's hot or not. He's a Fear."

I brushed a leaf from my hair and shielded my eyes from headlights as a car sped past. "Oh, wow. I can't believe you're going to bring up the Fear stuff. Do you like ancient history much?"

"It's not ancient history, Rach." Her green eyes flared. "There's a curse on the Fear family."

I laughed. I gave her a shove, making her stumble off the sidewalk. "Do you believe in vampires, too? Hey, look—two zombies just drove past in that car."

"You're so not funny, Rachel. Everyone in town knows about the Fears. And everyone knows the stories are true. The street that's named after them, Fear Street, where they all used to live. . . . You've heard the horrible things that happened there."

"Yes, everyone knows those old stories," I said, rolling my eyes.

She pulled up her jacket collar. "Listen to me, Rach. Brendan Fear's ancestors were witches or sorcerers or something. They had evil powers."

I laughed again. "Amy, give me a break. I really don't think Brendan Fear is a witch."

Her red lips formed a pout. "You just want to laugh at me. I'm trying to be your friend here. Am I stupid? Is that what you think? Go ahead. Tell me I'm stupid."

"No, you're not stupid," I said. "It's just—"

"Didn't we learn all those frightening stories about the Fears in school?" she interrupted as we crossed the street onto my block. "Remember? In sixth grade?"

"Amy, Mr. Gruder told us all those stories because it was Halloween. He was trying to scare us."

"Well, he scared *me*. And I believed them."

I didn't know what to say. I wished Amy would stop. I knew she was into fantasy novels, and she was always dragging me to horror movies. But I never thought she believed in all that spooky stuff.

Everyone in town knows the stories about the Fear family. But that all happened a long time ago. I mean, Brendan's father, Oliver Fear, is an investment banker, not an evil sorcerer. He's like a billionaire or something.

He built a huge stone mansion, totally awesome-looking,

with windows that reach up the whole side of the house, and waterfalls, and fountains all around. It's a tourist attraction. Seriously. People drive for miles to park in front of it and take pictures.

The moon drifted behind clouds as we crossed the street. Darkness washed over us. I felt a shiver run down my back. "I really think you're going overboard about the Fear family, Amy. Okay. Brendan is shy and he pretty much keeps to himself, and he's really into video games. That's no reason—"

"I just have a hunch," she said. "I have a very bad feeling about this. Rachel, you really want to be with Brendan Fear and his weird friends all night, all alone on that little island?"

I shrugged. "Seriously. What could happen?"

She shrugged. "Let's change the subject. Did you finally break up with Mac?"

I sighed. Thinking about Mac Garland made my stomach tighten. For weeks, I thought I really cared about him. Now I felt only dread when someone said his name. "I . . . I've given him lots of hints."

Amy frowned at me. "Hints? Like what?"

"Well . . . I changed my Facebook profile from *In a Relationship* to *It's Complicated.*"

"That's subtle."

"And I don't answer his texts or calls."

She stuck out an arm to block my path. "But you didn't just say it to him? You didn't say, I don't want to go out with you anymore?"

"Well . . ."

"You didn't say, get lost. Take a hike. Have a nice life. Go die."

"Huh? No. Of *course* not," I said. "Wow, Amy, you're really harsh tonight."

"You have to tell him," she said. "You have to confront him."

I shook my head. "I actually tried, but he . . . he got real scary. He started pounding his fist on the wall and cursing under his breath and . . . I really thought he might hurt me."

"Mac is a creep. I know I've asked you this before—but why did you start seeing him in the first place?"

I shrugged. "Because he asked me?"

Amy shook her head. "You just liked the idea of hanging with the bad boy. Someone dangerous."

"Yeah. Maybe I was bored. I admit it."

"Well, after Johnny Gruen, I don't blame you."

"Now you're going to dump on Johnny?"

"He's too boring to even discuss."

I laughed. "Just because he collects coins doesn't make him boring."

"Collecting coins doesn't make him boring. *Talking* about collecting coins makes him boring." Amy frowned.

"I thought we were discussing Mac. Are you really too afraid of him to tell him you're breaking up?"

"Well . . . a little bit, maybe. You know Mac. When he gets angry . . . sometimes he loses it."

Amy rolled her eyes. "Well, I can't tell him *for* you. I think—"

I didn't let her finish. I grabbed Amy's arm and let out a sharp cry. "Look!" I pointed.

Amy squinted into the darkness. "What is it? What's wrong?"

"My house. The front door. Amy, something's very wrong. The front door—it's wide open."

3.

MYSTERY OF THE OPEN DOOR

Relax, Rach. Maybe the wind—"

"No!" I cut her off. "You know my dad is a nut about locking the doors at night. He even makes sure the windows are locked."

I realized I was still gripping her arm. I let go and went running to the house. My shoes slid on the wet grass as I hurtled up the front yard.

I stopped on the front step and peered into the hall. Total darkness. As my eyes adjusted, I could see dim light washing in from the kitchen in the back. Dad always left a kitchen light on for me because I usually came in around the back.

I grabbed the railing and stared inside. My rapid breaths made puffs of steam rise in front of my face. Did someone break into our house?

I heard Amy step up behind me. "Rachel? You see anything?"

I shook my head. I stepped into the house. It was warm inside and smelled of the roast chicken my mother made for dinner. "Mom? Dad?" My voice came out in a hoarse whisper.

They weren't up. They've been going to bed earlier ever since Mom got Lyme disease.

My shoes scraped on the hardwood floor. I took a step, then another. I stopped and Amy bumped into me from behind.

"Oh. Sorry. Rachel, I don't hear anything. I think maybe . . ."

I clicked on a living room lamp. I guess I expected the room to be torn apart. I expected a prowler. Why else would the door be left wide open?

But everything seemed in its place. I saw two small ice-cream dishes on the side table next to the couch. My parents are ice-cream freaks. They are constantly trying new flavors. They talk about ice cream as if it's some kind of exotic gourmet treat.

My mom's glasses were on a couch cushion, next to a couple of magazines. "Everything seems okay," I whispered.

A sudden hum made me jump. It took me a few seconds to realize it was just the fridge starting up in the kitchen.

I tiptoed down the hall. Stopped outside the bathroom. Was the intruder lurking in there? I flashed on the light. The room was empty. No one in the kitchen, either.

The back of my neck tingled. A chill made my shoulders tighten.

Something is wrong. I feel it. Something has happened here.

"Amy, wait in the living room," I whispered. "I'm going to wake up my parents."

She nodded. "I think it was the wind, Rach. Really. Your parents are okay."

Her words didn't calm me down. I stepped into the back hall. Our house is ranch-style, all one floor. Their room was next to mine at the end of the hall. I was breathing hard as I reached their door. A ceiling light at the end of the hall sent pale yellow light over me.

Were they awake? I pressed my ear against the door and listened. Silence.

"Hey, Mom? Dad?" I said softly. I knocked with the knuckles on two fingers.

Silence.

Something horrible has happened to my parents.

"Mom? Dad?" I called, louder this time. I knocked harder, then didn't wait. I grabbed the knob, pushed the door open, and burst inside.

The room was dark. Gray light filtered in from the twin windows against the far wall. I heard a stirring. A groan.

"Rachel? Is that you?" Mom's voice, hoarse with sleep.

A bed table lamp flashed on. Dad lay on his side. He

turned and sat up blinking. Mom squinted at me, covers up to her chin.

"Rachel? What's wrong?" Dad asked.

"I . . . uh . . ." I hesitated for a moment. I felt a rush of relief seeing they were okay. "The front door . . ." I stammered finally. "It was open."

Dad scratched his balding head. He turned and started to climb out of bed. He's big. He looks like a bear with his furry chest. He sleeps only in pajama bottoms. "I know," he said. "I left it unlocked for you. In case you wanted to come in the front."

"You . . . you don't understand," I said. "It was wide open. The door was wide open."

"What?" Dad jumped to his feet. He squinted at me. "No way. I closed it carefully. I remember. I started to lock it. Then I changed my mind."

"Did you hear anything?" I asked. "Did you hear anyone come in or anything?"

"We went to bed early," Mom said. "I wasn't feeling very well, and—"

"I didn't hear anything," Dad said. "But, of course, I'm a heavy sleeper. Mom and I had a little wine with dinner and—"

"Rachel? Is everything okay?" Amy called from the front.

Dad blinked. "You didn't tell us anyone was here."

"It's just Amy," I said. I stepped into the hallway and called to her. "It's okay, Amy."

Dad shook his head. "There's no way that door could just fly open. Let me put my robe on, and I'll go check it."

I walked out into the hall and crossed to my room. I clicked on the ceiling light. The room looked just as I left it.

Was someone hiding in the closet? I hesitated for a few seconds, then slid the door open. My eyes glanced over the pile of dirty clothes I'd tossed on the closet floor. No. No one in there.

I returned to Amy in the living room. "False alarm," I said. "There's no intruder."

"It's way windy," she said. "I'll bet the wind did blow the door open."

Dad came bustling past me, tying the belt on his striped flannel robe. He nodded hello to Amy and stomped past her.

I followed him to the front door. He opened it and closed it several times. Then he scratched his stubbly face. "The latch is working okay. I don't get it."

"Well, at least no one broke in," Amy said.

Dad clicked the lock a few times. "Seems fine."

"I'd better go. It's late," Amy said.

I nodded. "Okay. Are you planning to continue your lecture about Brendan Fear tomorrow at school?"

"It wasn't a lecture, Rachel. I'm just trying to save you from a terrible weekend."

"Amy, you're not jealous, are you?" I said. "I don't know why I was invited, and you weren't."

She sighed. "Rachel, trust me. I'm not jealous. I'm just being smart. Even if the stories about the Fears are just folklore . . . folklore is based on something real . . . something that really happened."

Dad was still fiddling with the front door lock. His robe had come open, revealing a wide view of his hairy chest. Amy slipped past him onto the front stoop. "'Night. Catch you tomorrow." She turned and trotted down the front lawn.

Dad closed the door behind her. He clicked the lock. "Works fine." He scratched his stubbly chin again. "A mystery, I guess." He turned to me. "How was the restaurant?"

"Busy," I said. "I'm totally wrecked. And I smell like French fry grease. Goodnight. I need a very long shower and shampoo."

But when I got into my room, I dropped onto the edge of my bed, yawning. My legs ached from standing for so many hours. My back hurt, too. I decided if I took a shower now it might wake me up. And I wanted to go straight to sleep.

I tossed my clothes on the floor and pulled on a long

nightshirt. Then I clicked off the ceiling light and moved through the darkness to my bed.

I couldn't stop yawning. I'd never felt so weary and exhausted. I pulled the covers back and slid into bed. The sheets felt cozy and warm. I slid lower in the bed.

My right foot bumped something under the covers. My toes rubbed against something lumpy and hard. Prickly fur tickled the bottom of my foot.

At first I thought it was just a wrinkle in the sheet or blanket. But my foot pressed against it. It felt hard. Furry and hard.

My breath caught in my throat. I pulled myself up. Flashed on the bed table lamp. Slid my feet out. Some dark fur was stuck to my toes.

"Huh?" I jumped out of bed and jerked the covers down.

And opened my mouth in a scream of horror as I stared at the dead, decaying rat in my bed.

4.

IS MAC A PSYCHO?

I knew it was Mac. It had to be Mac.

What a childish and obnoxious way to pay me back for dumping him. He crept into our house through the front door and slipped the rat in my bed. What a psycho. What a sociopath.

Mac transferred to Shadyside High last year. I knew he had a bad reputation. I heard he'd been suspended from his old school for fighting. I'd seen his violent temper.

But I also thought he was a good guy at heart. He was kind at times and very soft-spoken, even shy. He had a tender side he didn't let many people see. Yes, he was very possessive, even though we'd only been seeing each other for a few weeks. And he resented the time I spent with Amy and my other friends.

But I kind of thought that meant he cared.

Stupid me.

Amy warned me about him right from the start. She

said I was just looking for the opposite to my old boyfriend. She didn't like Mac's bursts of anger, the way he started to curse and carry on at the tiniest frustration. The way he always tried to act tougher than everyone else.

Now Mac was obviously out to prove Amy right.

Okay. Okay. He was angry that I stopped answering his calls or his texts. That I ignored him when he tried to stop me at school. That I changed my Facebook page and told everyone that he and I were over.

Angry enough to sneak into my house and tuck a dead rat in my bed.

Sick. Totally sick.

My room became a blur. I focused on the darkness outside my window. Stared hard and tried to slow my rapid heartbeats.

Mom and Dad must have heard my scream. They came bursting into my room. Mom's hair was wild about her head. It looked like a tossed-up ocean wave. They both came in blinking and muttering. But their eyes went wide when they saw the dead creature stretched out on its side on my sheets.

"Ohhh." Mom covered her mouth and made a gagging sound.

Dad stepped up to the bed and stared down as if he'd never seen a rat before. "How . . . how did this get here?" He turned to me. "Do you think the open door . . . ?" His voice trailed off. He knew that was crazy.

"I don't know," I said. I didn't want to accuse Mac. I didn't want to get into the whole thing.

My parents are good, understanding people. But ever since I was little, I've always preferred to keep things to myself and deal with them on my own. Even when I was a little kid, I didn't want to share what I'd done in school that day. I guess I'm weird that way. And, of course, I always had Beth to confide in. I always felt more comfortable telling things to my sister.

Mom turned so she wouldn't have to look at the rat. She's the squeamish one in our family. "Probably came from your closet," she said. "I've been telling you it's a rat's nest."

"Is that supposed to be a joke?" I snapped.

She shook her head. "No. I'm serious. That mountain of dirty clothes . . ."

"I'll call the exterminator in the morning," Dad said.

"I have to get out of here," Mom said. Her whole body shuddered. She hugged the front of her nightgown. "The smell . . . it's making me sick. Rachel, do you want to come to the kitchen and have some tea or something?"

"No," I said. I sighed. "I just want to get to sleep. I'm so tired, I want to cry."

"I'll get some gloves and carry the rat out to the garbage," Dad said. "Then we can change the sheets." He shook his head. "I still don't understand. . . ."

"Me neither," I said softly.

But I thought, *Mac, you can frighten me. But you can't ruin my life. I'm going to Brendan Fear's birthday party. It's going to be the greatest all-night party ever. Brendan invited me, and I'm going. You're history, Mac. I'm just glad I found out what a psycho you are. Really. I'm glad.*

5.

THE GAME

On Friday morning, I came to school early, hoping to catch Mac before homeroom. But he didn't show. He wasn't at school all day. And he didn't answer his phone or reply to my texts.

I just wanted to tell him what a jerk he was. I wanted to tell him he was lucky I didn't call the police or tell my parents.

I didn't want to make a deal out of it. I just wanted to let him know how sick he was. I'd been afraid to face him, to tell him it was over between us. But now he'd made it totally easy.

Mac wasn't around, so I put him out of my mind. I thought about Brendan and the party instead. *What should I wear? Why did Brendan invite me? Could he maybe have a thing about me? Who else is going?*

Maybe I thought about Brendan *too* much. Amy poked me during Creative Writing class after lunch and said,

"Get that dreamy look off your face. You could be arrested for looking that happy."

I wasn't into basketball. But Amy and I had planned all week to meet in the gym to watch the Shadyside Tigers play the St. Ignatius Sharks.

She said we should go because it was our last basketball homecoming game. And even though we weren't really basketball fans, it was a kind of milestone, maybe something we'd remember years later.

Amy is so weird. It's like she's always living her life in the future. She thinks a lot about what we'll remember twenty years from now.

So, a little after seven thirty, I pushed open the double doors and stepped into the gym. Despite the roar of voices and the steady thump of basketballs on the floor as the teams did their warm-ups, the shouts and laughs ringing off the tile walls, and the shrill *blaat* of a trumpet player goofing around in the band across the floor, I suddenly found myself thinking about Mac. . . . Mac and that disgusting dead rat.

I didn't want to, but I suddenly felt angry all over again.

Beth flashed into my mind. If only Beth were around. She was so smart and had such common sense. She would know how to help me get calm. Beth would say, "Get over it, Rachel. You're done with that creep. Just wipe him from your mind."

I let out a long sigh and gazed around the crowded gym. It was close to game time and the bleachers were already jammed to the top. I stood by the steps at the side and searched row by row for Amy. Then I remembered I had gotten a text from her. She was having some problem with her parents and said she might be late.

I climbed to the next-to-the-top row and slid onto the bench. I pulled off my hoodie and put it down beside me to save a seat for Amy. Down on the floor, the hoops were ringing with the sound of guys throwing in layups. The Sharks were practicing at the other side of the court. Their uniforms were gray and black. Shark colors, I guess.

On our side, I saw Kerry Reacher bending, stretching his leg muscles. Kerry was about a foot taller than everyone else on the Tigers. Our team had a three-and-six record. Major fail. But everyone knew that Kerry was going to be named All-State again this year.

I searched the bleachers for Mac. But I knew he wouldn't be here. He never came to any games.

I turned to see Eric Finn bounce onto the bench beside me. I shoved him. "Hey, you're sitting on my hoodie."

"I know," he said, grinning his toothy grin right in my face. "The wood bench is too hard."

"But I'm saving the seat for somebody," I said, tugging the sleeve of the hoodie. No way I could pull it out from under the big dude.

"Saving it for me?" he said. "Thanks. I didn't know you cared."

"I'm crazy about you," I said. "But I'm saving the seat for Amy."

"If she comes, you can sit here." He patted his lap. He was kind of cute with all those freckles on his big round baby face. He jumped up and shouted to some guys down near the floor. I saw Patti Berger in the second row. She was with her friend April Conklin. They were both watching Kerry intently as he practiced free throws.

Eric gave me a poke in the ribs with his elbow. "Guess you're dying to hang with me at Brendan's party. I might let you, if you beg."

He was leaning his heavy shoulder on me. I pushed him upright. "Have you been to his birthday parties before? You have, right?"

"Yeah. They're awesome," he said. He brushed back his wavy blond hair. "Totally wild. I mean, like out of control."

I laughed. "What *do* you mean?"

He leaned on me again. "You know. You know what happens when a bunch of us spend the night together and there are no parents around."

"You mean it's *that* kind of party?"

"You can never predict Brendan. He always has some surprises. You know. He's the game master. We all bow down to his brilliance." He bowed down and nearly fell onto the row of seats in front of us.

I laughed. "You know what your problem is. You're way too serious. You should lighten up."

"Everyone tells me that."

The next question just blurted from my mouth. "Why do you think Brendan invited me to his birthday party? I've seen him around school forever. But we're not really friends."

Eric pinched my nose. "I think he likes you."

"Huh?" I shoved his hand away. "What do you mean? How do you know?"

He shrugged. "He told me."

"He *told* you what? What did he say?" Why was my heart flip-flopping in my chest?

A sly grin spread over Eric's chubby face. "What's it worth to you?"

"Don't be a jerk, Eric. Tell me what he said."

"We passed you in the hall, after Earth Sciences. Brendan said he wanted to jump you right there in the hall. He said you were the hottest, most awesome girl in school."

I shoved him again. "You idiot."

"Okay. Well, he didn't exactly say that. He said he liked you. At least, I *think* it was you. There were a whole bunch of girls in the hall. Now that I think about it, it was probably someone else."

I shook my head. "You're making it all up. You're such a liar, Eric."

"I know. But I'm cute. Right?"

I turned away from him, thinking about Brendan. Maybe he just invited me on an impulse because he saw me in Lefty's. Or maybe he really did like me. No way I'd get a straight answer from Eric.

A buzzer rang out, echoing off the tile walls of the gym. The teams stopped their practice shots and trotted to the benches at the sidelines. Two referees in black-and-white striped shirts moved to the center of the court.

I heard musical chimes. It took me a few seconds to realize that my phone was ringing. I dug it out of my hoodie pocket and raised the screen to my face.

Amy calling.

"Amy? Hi. Where are you? The game is starting."

"Forget the game," Amy said. "I can't come. I've been grounded. My stupid parents are acting stupid again."

"Why? What happened?"

The crowd suddenly jumped to their feet and roared. The Tigers came trotting to the center of the floor. I couldn't hear Amy's answer.

"Can I come over?" I shouted, pressing the phone hard to my ear. "Is it okay if I come over?"

"You'll miss the game."

"I don't care about the game," I said. "See you in a few minutes."

I jumped up and tried to squeeze past Eric. But he

grabbed me around the waist and pulled me onto his lap. "Rachel, you know you're crazy about me. Why are you fighting it?"

I patted his cheek. "Do you want to be my date for Brendan's party?"

He laughed. "Not really."

I pulled myself to my feet and scooted to the aisle. "See you tomorrow," I called to Eric. But he was already talking to the girl next to him.

The whistle blew and the game started. I stepped along the edge of the playing floor, pushing open the double doors, and walked into the hall. The roar faded behind me as the gym doors closed.

I was thinking about Amy as I walked to the back of the school. The hall was empty. Everyone was in the gym watching the game. Amy's parents were always on her case. She never wanted to say why. She always said they were stupid. I knew they fought all the time. And it never seemed it was about anything important.

I was there one afternoon when Amy's mom told her she needed a total attitude adjustment. Amy just stared at her, and said, "*You're* the one with the attitude. Not me."

That got Amy grounded for a week.

Pretty stupid.

I stepped out onto the student parking lot in back of the school. It was a clear, cold night. I could see my breath puff in front of me. The parking lot was jammed with cars. The streetlights made the cars gleam almost as bright as day.

I saw my white Camry across two aisles. Shivering from the damp cold, I pulled my hoodie tighter. I tugged the key from my bag. I was a few feet from the car door when I heard running footsteps on the asphalt.

Before I could turn, strong hands grabbed my shoulders roughly from behind.

I gasped and tried to pull free.

But my attacker held on and, with a grunt, spun me around.

"Mac!" I choked out. "Mac—what are you doing? Let go of me! Mac—what are you *doing*? Let *go*!"

6.

"I HEARD THINGS I SHOULDN'T"

just want to talk," he said, pressing my back against the car. "Can we just talk?"

"Talk? Are you crazy?" I cried. "Get your hands off me. Now."

He lowered his hands but didn't step back. His cold, gray eyes locked on mine. His blondish hair glowed under the light.

I shook myself, like a dog trying to shake off fleas. I could still feel his grip on my shoulders. "You scare me to death and you want to talk?" I said. "After what you did last night?"

His hands whipped the air. "Listen to me, Rachel. Just listen to me."

My heart was pounding. I'd seen him go from calm to furious in two seconds. It was terrifying to watch. What could I do to keep him from exploding?

I stared hard at him, alert to any move he might make, stared as if I'd never really seen him before. Mac is good-looking. Amy says he looks like a young Brad Pitt, and I guess he does.

He doesn't smile very much. And he has this weird tic where he blinks three or four times in a few seconds. Like a twitch. It doesn't happen very often, but I think it shows how tense he is.

He wore a faded army-green jacket over a black T-shirt and skinny-legged jeans torn at both knees and black boots. I glimpsed a wrinkled pack of cigarettes in a pocket of his jacket.

"Mac," I whispered. "Go away. I don't ever want to talk to you. After last night—"

"Last night I was crazy," he said. "I was out of my mind. Rachel, I spent all last night, the whole night, in my car. I was so messed up about you. I was up all night. I couldn't come to school today. I thought . . . I thought . . . you and I. We . . ."

"No, Mac," I said. "We're over. I'm sorry. But you've got to deal with it. We're over. How can you even think I will talk to you? After . . . after the dead rat."

He blinked. "The what?"

"The dead rat."

"Rachel, what are you talking about?"

"Oh, don't try to lie to me," I said. "You're such a bad liar, Mac. Why do you even try?"

Whenever Mac tells a lie, these round pink spots appear on his cheeks. And they were definitely there now. I could see them even in the pale light of the parking lot.

I grabbed my car door. "Please—let me go. Let's just say good-bye, okay? Just back off and let me go."

"I . . . can't," he said. He didn't budge. Again, those silvery eyes burned into mine. "I have to tell you something, Rachel. Something else. Not about you and me. You have to listen to me."

"If I listen quietly, will you let me go? Do you promise?"

He nodded. "Yeah. Sure. But you've got to listen. I . . . saw you talking to Brendan Fear."

"So?" I said. "You were spying on me?"

"You have to stay away from him."

"Excuse me? I don't think so, Mac. I can talk to anyone I want." My voice cracked. I didn't want to provoke him. I didn't want to set off his anger.

He kicked one of my tires with his boot. "Listen. I'm serious. Rachel, don't go to Fear Island. Don't go to that party."

"How do you know I was invited? How do you know my private conversations? Listen to me, Mac. You and I— we're over. Do you get it? Over. So you have to stop stalking me and spying on me. And you can't tell me who I can see and who I can't."

He shook his head. "Just don't go, Rachel. I . . . I've heard things."

"Heard things? Are you crazy?" My voice came out high and shrill.

He grabbed my arms again. He squeezed them, so tight I cried out. "Mac, get off. You're hurting me."

"I heard things, Rachel. I heard things I shouldn't."

"Mac—let go of me. I'm warning you. Mac, you've got to get help. You're out of control. You have got to get help before you do something terrible."

"Don't go. Hear me? It's for your own good." He started to shake me.

"Stop!" I screamed. I spun around and tugged my arms free. I gave him a hard shove that sent him stumbling backward. He lost his balance and landed on his butt on the asphalt.

Gasping for breath, I moved fast. I pulled open the car door and slid inside. I slammed it shut and locked the doors.

I could still hear Mac shouting as I started the car and backed out of the space. In the rearview mirror, I saw him still on the ground, shaking a fist at me.

"I'm warning you," he rasped. "Warning you, Rachel. Stay away from Fear Island. Stay away from Brendan Fear."

I roared off, nearly clipping the bumper of the car at the end of the row. I squealed into the turn as I bumped onto the street.

"Good-bye, Mac," I said out loud. "Good-bye, Mac." I

gunned the car and tore away, away from him, away from all his craziness. "Good-bye, Mac. And good riddance."

But was that the end of my frightening troubles with Mac?

If only.

7.

"BE AFRAID, RACHEL"

My dreams are always very ordinary, and I *never* have nightmares. A while ago, I had my scariest dream ever. Beth and I were shopping at a clothing store and I got lost and couldn't find her.

Big whoop, right?

The truth is, I almost never remember my dreams in the morning. I guess because they're so dull.

But the night before Brendan Fear's birthday party, I had the weirdest, most terrifying dream I ever had. This dream was so strange and upsetting, I woke up with it vivid in my mind.

The dream took place in a thick forest or woods. Flashes of bright sunlight kept poking through the trees, making it hard to see. I watched myself wandering through the woods, wandering aimlessly. Until I saw an injured bird on the ground.

It was dark brown with scraggly feathers. It was cheep-

48

ing softly, almost mournfully, tucked in on itself because it was in pain. I picked it up in both hands and tried to comfort it. As I petted its back, the bird slowly began to change.

I had it cupped in my hands. I watched it change shape, stretch out, grow a hairy snout. The bird in my hand became a *rat*. I tried to drop it but it stuck to my hands. I tried to toss it away, but the rat wouldn't budge.

Then I cried out in shock as the rat suddenly had a human face. A man's face. It opened its mouth, and I saw long, curled fangs. They glimmered like ivory. The rat made a shrill hissing sound and sank its long teeth into my wrist.

I screamed as bright red blood gushed up from my arm like a fountain. The rat disappeared in the flowing curtain of red. I saw only red. Then it vanished. I was standing in the woods. I had a feeling I wasn't alone. Someone was watching me from the trees. But the sunlight was so bright, I couldn't see.

Then the sunlight faded, and I saw Brendan Fear. He stood very close. I started to move toward him. But I stopped when he tossed back his head and began to laugh. Horrible, crazy laughter. Cruel laughter.

And as he laughed, he suddenly had a rat's face. The rat laughed and laughed. I wanted to get away from Brendan. I remember trying to wake up, trying to pull myself up from the dream. But I was stuck there. I couldn't escape.

Brendan's rat face opened its mouth. It had curled fangs, dripping with blood. I turned and ran, ran through the dark trees. Brendan chased after me. The cold, cruel laughter followed me. I ran and ran, but I couldn't outrun him.

Suddenly, I knew the trees were all alive. They were alive and watching me. It was some kind of a trap. I knew I would never escape. The dark trees wriggled and shook. They started to slide toward me across the ground. A horrible wrenching sound rang in my ears as the trees uprooted themselves one by one and moved in on me.

Brendan grabbed me from behind. He whirled me around. He had his human face back, not a rat face. He pulled me close. His cheeks pressed against mine. His face felt so cold, cold as death.

And he whispered in my ear: "Be afraid, Rachel."

I woke up shaking, my pillow drenched with sweat. The dream played back in my mind. I remembered every second of it, every horrifying second.

I jumped out of bed. I stumbled to my bedroom window. I wanted to get as far away from that dream as I could.

I had no way of knowing the nightmare had just begun.

PART
TWO

8.

A CHILL

Even though it's a short boat ride, I'd never been to Fear Island. I've heard kids talk about it. It's an almost perfectly round island of thick woods, dirt roads, and little summer cabins along its shore. It stands in the middle of Fear Lake, too far out to be seen from the town side of the lake.

On Saturday afternoon, my dad drove me to the dock at the end of Fear Street. It was a gray day threatening rain, but there was no way the weather could dampen my excitement.

I had changed my outfit three times before I left the house, ending up with some really tight black jeans that had cost me a week's salary, my favorite shoes, and a camisole covered by a chic short tangerine-colored jacket my aunt had sent me from New York.

I kissed Dad's cheek and slid out of the car. I could see

some kids stepping into a double-decker white catamaran that bobbed beside the dock.

I started to trot toward them when I heard Dad's voice from the car. "Rachel? Forget something?" He held up my backpack.

Guess I was a little nervous.

I grabbed it from him, slung it over my shoulder, and jogged to the dock. I had no idea what I'd packed in the bag. Brendan said the party would go all night, so there was no need to bring a nightshirt or pajamas or anything. I tossed in some lipsticks and a blusher and a hairbrush and a bottle of water and I-don't-know-what-else. It all made a rattling sound as the backpack bounced on my shoulder.

The lake shimmered in shades of dark green, reflecting the dark skies up above, and low whitecaps washed against the pilings along the short wooden dock. The catamaran had two windowed decks top and bottom, and looked like a big sleek yacht. I was expecting a rowboat or something with an outboard motor, but this was much cooler.

It rocked gently, bumping the dock with soft thuds. Seagulls squawked and chattered from the top of a tele-phone pole at the street.

A twenty-something dude, dressed in white, with a white admiral's cap trimmed in gold tilted over his tanned face, stood at the edge of the dock, helping kids step down into the boat. I watched him hold Patti Berger's hand as she lowered herself from the dock.

He nodded as I walked up to him. He had nice blue eyes and a friendly smile. "I'm Randy," he said. "I'm the pilot. You can sit wherever you like."

"Awesome tan," I said.

"Thanks." He pushed the cap back so I could see it better. "I was sailing off Eleuthra in the Bahamas."

"Sweet," I said. A tall wave rocked the boat as I stepped off the dock, and I nearly fell. He grabbed my arm to steady me.

"Not a good day for a swim," I said. I flashed him a teasing grin. "Would you dive in and pull me out if I fell in?"

"Want to see?" He motioned to the water. "Go ahead. Jump in."

The dare stood between us for a few seconds. *Was he teasing?* Of course he was.

"Maybe on the way back," I said.

I saw seven or eight kids already on the boat, sitting on the white benches along the sides of the deck. There were four rows of benches in the center facing the bow, but they were empty except for two guys in jeans and brown leather jackets.

I didn't recognize them. They were sort of glum looking, mumbling to each other, dark hair falling over their foreheads, hands deep in their jacket pockets, ignoring the others.

The boat rocked hard again. This time, I kept my balance. I dropped down next to Patti. As always, she looked like a little doll. She was wearing a short, shiny gray skirt over black jeans. Her parka was open, revealing a violet vest over a pale blue T-shirt. She had plastic yellow-and-blue beads around her neck that clattered when she moved.

"That skirt is nice," I said. "Is it silk?"

"Silk*ish*," she said. We both laughed.

I glanced around. "Where's Kerry?"

Patti rolled her eyes. "Late as usual."

A seagull soared low over the boat, squawking loudly, searching for food. The sky darkened as storm clouds slid together.

I glanced around, checking out the other kids.

April Conklin turned and waved at me. She is short and thin and looks about twelve instead of sixteen. She has straight black hair down to her shoulders, dark eyes behind the red-framed glasses she always wears, a beautiful smile. She was wearing skinny, low-rise jeans, brown boots, and two T-shirts, a pale blue shirt over a white shirt.

April is a serious cellist. She plays in the Shadyside Youth Symphony, and she has a scholarship to be a music major at Dartmouth next year. She's majorly talented, but she's too modest to ever talk about it. She and my sister got to be friends since they are both serious musicians.

Across the deck, I saw Delia Rodgers and Geena Steves. Delia is a funny girl with very short white-blonde hair, light blue eyes, a lot of dark eye makeup around them, and at least five rings in each ear. She has a flower tattoo on one ankle and another one on her back that she says her parents will kill her for if they ever see it.

Delia can be kind of tough. Last year, she got into a hair-pulling, drag-out fight at a basketball game with a girl from Martin's Landing. She was suspended from school for a week. She told everyone it was totally worth it. Ever since, people have been careful around Delia.

Delia's thumbs were furiously tapping at her phone. She didn't even look up when Geena said something to her.

Geena is tall and thin and pretty, with creamy white skin and dark brown eyes and wavy copper-colored hair down to her shoulders.

Her father owns the Chevrolet dealership in Waynesville, and he uses Geena in his TV commercials because she's so beautiful. Geena takes classes at an acting school and says she auditions for other TV commercials all the time.

She and I were good friends when we were little. But we drifted apart when we got to middle school. No reason. We still like each other.

She was talking to Robby Webb. Robby joined our

class last year. I don't know where he went to school before. Robby is African American, tall, and very skinny, with big, dark eyes and a great friendly smile. He told everyone to call him Spider. Spider Webb.

He seems like a nice guy, but no one really knows him that well. He works at the Dairy Queen after school, and he doesn't go to any games or dances or school things.

"I thought there'd be more kids," I told Patti.

She was texting someone on her phone. Probably Kerry. Probably asking where he was. She finished and looked up. "Yeah, it's a small party. You never can predict Brendan. He's so weird."

"Do you really think he's weird?"

She shrugged. "Actually, I think he's way smarter than most people. His mind—it just shoots off in a million directions. Kerry hangs out with him a lot more than I do. He says Brendan is *obsessed* with all the games he plays. Like he lives in a game world."

She glanced at her phone screen, then turned back to me. "You and Brendan—I didn't know you were friends."

I shook my head. "We're not. I don't really know why I was invited."

She smiled. "Maybe Brendan has a thing for you."

"Maybe." I laughed. "And maybe I'll flap my arms and fly to Mars."

"No. Really. It's possible," she insisted.

Eric Finn appeared, bouncing toward us, imitating the

seagull that kept flying over us, squawking at it. Some kids squawked back at him.

Eric plopped down heavily beside me. He tossed his bulging backpack on the cabin floor and turned to Patti and me. "Hey, sorry to keep you girls waiting. Were you worried about me?"

"No," Patti and I answered in unison.

"Well, I'm here. The party can start." He grinned at me. "You probably shouldn't sit next to me, Rachel."

"Why not?"

"I get real seasick. Seriously. Even on a lake."

"Thanks for the warning," I said. "You're joking, right? I can never tell with you."

"I'm serious. I do a lot of major-league projectile vomiting on boats. I'll try not to get any on you. Too bad I had a huge lunch." He tugged the sleeve of my jacket. "Hey, good thing you wore a vomit-colored jacket."

I jerked my arm away. "It's not vomit-colored, idiot. It's tangerine. And stop stretching it."

"Did you take anything for seasickness?" Patti asked him.

Eric nodded. "My dad gave me a meclizine. I think it's making me dizzy. Whoa!" He made a swooning sound and fell over on me, dropping his head in my lap.

Patti laughed. Spider and Geena laughed, too. "Don't encourage him," I said. I shoved him off me. "You are *so* not funny."

"Face it, you can't keep your hands off me, can you?" Eric said. "You want me, don't you!"

"Yes, I want you. I want you to *leave*."

He made a snorting sound. He pinched the sleeve of my jacket. "I had gym socks this color."

"Give Rachel a break," Patti said. "It's an awesome jacket. I think she looks great."

"Why did you leave the basketball game so quickly last night?" Eric asked. "Was it because I forgot to wear deodorant yesterday?"

"Do you always answer your own questions?" I replied. "Let's just say that sitting next to you, I was emotionally overcome."

"I do that to people," Eric said, grinning. "Wish your friend Amy was invited to the party." He gazed around at the other guests.

"Why?" I said.

"Because she's totally hot."

I wished Amy was here, too. I was excited to be going to this party, but I was also nervous. I promised myself that I would stop trying to figure out why I was invited and just enjoy the party, but that would have been so much easier if my best friend was with me . . .

Eric suddenly jumped to his feet. "Hey," he shouted, "does the orgy start on the boat, or do we have to keep our clothes on till we get to Brendan's house?"

That got some laughs and hoots. Someone tossed an

empty Coke can at Eric. It bounced off his shoulder and rolled across the deck.

The boat engine started up with a low roar.

Randy appeared and waved his admiral's cap above his head for attention. "Okay, everyone," he called, "sit down, please. We're moving now. The lake is a little choppy today, so—"

Patti and I interrupted him with a shout. We saw Kerry Reacher running full speed toward the boat, his backpack flying behind him. "Wait for Kerry!" Patti cried.

Kerry did a wild leap off the dock, his long legs scissoring the air. He landed on the deck, waving his arms above his head to get his balance. A perfect landing.

Everyone cheered.

"Slam dunk," Kerry said, pushing his hands up as if shooting a basket.

More cheers.

Randy pulled off his cap and scratched his brown hair. "Okay. Guess everyone is here. Let's shove off. If you need me, I'll be up there." He pointed to the wheel at the top cabin.

Kerry squeezed between me and Patti. That put me practically in Eric's lap. "Rachel, I knew it," Eric said. "You can't keep your hands off me." He rubbed his hand up and down the sleeve of my jacket.

I gave him a shove. "Aren't you seasick yet? Why don't you go lean over the rail? Lean real far over."

"Rachel, don't try to hide your true feelings."

We both laughed. Eric wasn't as funny as he thought he was, but he was still pretty funny.

The engine roared again. The boat rocked hard, then started to move. Eric turned to talk to April, who sat on his other side. "Did you bring your cello?"

She laughed. "What do *you* think?"

"Do you remember Brendan's tenth birthday?" Kerry asked. "It was awesome. His parents turned their whole backyard into an amusement park. Brendan Land. Really. They had a real roller coaster."

Eric grinned. "I was there. They had Dodge Em cars, too. Were you at his beach party two years ago? They had fireworks, and we went swimming in the lake at midnight."

April nodded. "It was so beautiful. They had those floats with lanterns all lit up across the water."

Eric grinned at her. "I remember you and Danny Goldman went off down the beach together, and no one could find you, and we thought we'd have to call the Coast Guard or something."

April blushed bright red. "Shut up, Eric."

Everyone laughed.

I felt a sudden chill.

The lake air was cool. But it wasn't that kind of chill. My whole body shivered.

Sometimes I have these feelings. Premonitions, I guess.

Nothing special. I think everyone has them. You know like how sometimes you just *know* that someone is watching you. And then it turns out to be true.

Seagulls squawked and darted overhead, as if leading the way to the island. Their cries rose over the hum of the boat engine.

"Hey, Rachel." April leaned over Eric to talk to me. "What's up with you and Mac?"

"We broke up," I said. "Actually, I broke up with him. Why?"

"Well, I just saw him. I thought maybe he was coming to the party with you."

"You *what*?" I jumped to my feet. "You *saw* him?"

I turned toward the shore. The boat was moving steadily away. But I squinted over the green glare off the water and saw someone. Someone half-hidden behind the telephone pole at the road. He stood with one arm around the pole, watching the boat, watching me.

Mac. I recognized him even at this distance.

Mac watching me.

Spying on me.

"Rachel? Are you okay?" April's voice broke into my thoughts. She stared at me. "You have the strangest look on your face."

"Oh. Uh . . . no biggie," I said, my eyes on Mac. "I just felt a chill."

9.

BLOOD IN THE WATER

The storm clouds slid apart as we neared Fear Island, and rays of yellow sunlight slanted down on the bare trees. Shielding my eyes with one hand, I could see a couple of small summer cottages, boarded up for winter, with their tiny docks empty.

I'm going to have an awesome time, I told myself. *I've left Mac behind and I'm going to a party in an island mansion, and stay up all night, and make new friends, and maybe get close to Brendan Fear, and have a total blast.*

And somehow . . . this time I really believed it.

As Randy guided the boat around the curve of the island, the Fear house came into view, rising above the trees like a dark tower. Brendan's house was *not* a summer cottage. It looked more like a castle. It was at least three stories high, built of black stone that glowed under the sunlight, tall windows, all dark, a slanting red roof with

chimneys poking up all up and down its length, and balconies that jutted out toward the trees.

I really am entering a different world, I thought, gazing over
the glare of the water at the incredible mansion.

"Cute little cottage," Patti said, snapping a photo with
her phone. "Think there's enough room for a party?"

"I've lived in Shadyside my whole life, but I've never
seen this place," I said. "I knew the Fears were rich. But I
never imagined . . ."

The boat rocked in the water, slowing as we approached
the wooden dock. I turned to Eric. "You and Brendan
come here a lot, right?"

He nodded. "Yeah. Believe it or not, that humongous
castle is just Brendan's summer house. They closed it up
in September. Brendan and I hang here a lot. It's seriously
boring."

"Boring?"

"There's no Internet. No WiFi. No bars on your phone.
It's like . . . welcome to caveman days."

I laughed. "That could be a good thing."

A gust of wind blew his hair straight up on his head.
"It's a good place to film a horror movie," he said, pushing the wild tuft of hair back down with one hand. "Big
rooms filled with heavy, old furniture. Long dark halls
twisting this way and that. It's supposed to be a summer
house. But the whole place is dark and depressing."

He pointed. "See all those huge windows? I mean, even when it's sunny out, the light doesn't seem to come in."

"Weird."

His eyes grew wide. "There are long, creepy shadows everywhere. And the shadows seem to move on their own. And I'm always hearing horrible howls from up in the attic."

I laughed. "Now you're just trying to scare me—aren't you?"

He grinned. "You think so?"

The boat bumped hard against the wooden dock. A few kids cried out in surprise. Eric pretended to fall off his seat and landed on his butt on the deck. He really is like a five-year-old. He's kind of cute, but he's a big baby. And he always has to be the center of attention.

Kerry helped pull him to his feet. Randy leaped onto the dock and tied the catamaran to the pilings. We scrambled to climb off. The spray from the lake air made my face feel cold and damp. I took a deep breath and inhaled a wonderful sweet aroma from the trees.

"See you guys later," Randy said, helping April off the boat. "Antonio and Miguel will guide you up to the house."

Antonio was a tall, lean young man with tiny dark eyes, a sharp nose, a shiny round stud in one nostril, and black hair pulled behind his head in a ponytail that fell down his back.

Miguel was older, shorter, and pudgy, an African American with a broad forehead and a lot of white in his hair.
They both were in uniform—black dress shirt, black tie,
and black slacks. They both had little white nametags on
their shirt pockets.

"They must be new," Eric whispered in my ear. "I
haven't seen either of them before. The Fears have *so many*
people working for them."

"But the house has been closed, right?" I said. "They
just opened it for Brendan's party today."

Eric nodded. He darted over to Geena and put his arm
around her. "I see you watching me, Geena. You can't
take your eyes off me, can you? Maybe you and I can sneak
away later. Maybe do some nature walks on the island?
Are you into nature like I am?"

She laughed. "That's a maybe, Eric."

"You mean it's a *yes*?"

Geena shook her head. "A *maybe* is a *no*."

"So it's a yes," Eric said.

"No."

"I'll take that to be a yes."

The sky darkened again, and the air grew cooler. Behind
us, the boat rose up, then splashed down as waves washed
hard against the narrow dock.

"Okay, guys. Let's get to the house before the rain
comes," Antonio shouted. He had some kind of foreign
accent. Italian, I think. He pointed to a dirt path that led

through the tall grass, away from the shore. "It's a short hike through the woods. Be careful to stay on the path. There are a lot of snakes."

"What kind of snakes?" Patti asked.

"The kind you don't want to meet," Antonio replied.

We all started toward the path. I stopped when I heard a shrill scream.

I turned back in time to see Randy fall. One foot was caught in the tie rope, and he screamed again as he stumbled off the dock. I gasped as his head hit one of the tall log pilings. It made a sick *thud*.

His white cap landed upside down on the dock. Arms slumped at his sides, Randy dropped into the churning lake water.

Screaming, shouting in shock, we went running to the dock. Antonio and Miguel were already on their knees, peering into the water. They tried to wave us back. "He'll be okay," Antonio shouted. "He's a good swimmer."

"Back, everyone," Miguel ordered. "Get back."

No one moved. My heart was pounding in my chest. I struggled to catch my breath.

And then I uttered a choked cry as a circle of bright red rose up in the dark lapping water. The red tint spread quickly, washing with the waves.

"Blood! It's his blood!" Geena shouted.

"Where *is* he? Why isn't he coming up?" Delia cried.

I'd been holding my breath the whole time. I forced

myself to breathe. My legs suddenly felt weak. No sign of him.

Antonio began to wave frantically. "Get up to the house! All of you! Miguel—take them to the house. I'll deal with this. Everyone—*move!*" He tugged his shoes off, then started to strip off his clothes.

"He'll be okay. Randy'll be okay," Miguel kept repeating. He frantically began moving us off the dock. "Come on, everybody. Antonio will pull him out. No worries. Really. No worries."

I had no choice. I had to follow the others to the path that led to the house. But as I stepped off the dock, I turned back. And saw the water so crimson, rippling red, the blood spreading in the waves and around the dock. And no sign of Randy . . . just Randy's blood, billowing up from down below.

10.

ROADKILL

I shut my eyes. I turned away from the horrifying sight at the dock.

Was it really possible? Was the party ruined by a drowning before it even began?

I suddenly thought about Amy. She warned me not to come to this party. She kept saying there was a curse on the Fear family. Mac warned me, too, but he was crazy and jealous and out of control.

"Keep moving, everyone," Miguel ordered us. "Don't worry about Randy. Antonio has it all under control." His voice trembled. It was obvious Miguel was lying.

"Is Randy okay?" I cried. "Did Antonio pull him out?"

"It's under control," Miguel repeated. "Let's all move now."

I felt sick. I decided to text Amy and tell her maybe she was right about this party. I pulled out my phone. No bars. Of course. Eric warned me that phones wouldn't work on the island.

The path sloped up as we approached the house. I heard a strange bird cry from a high tree limb. A long *Hoo-hoooo*. So sad and human. Like someone crying. My nightmare flashed into my mind. The little brown bird on the grass that became a rat in my hands. The deep bite of its fangs. The blood gushing from my wrist.

No. *Stop, Rachel. Get that nightmare out of your head. Think about Brendan. He invited you because he likes you. Think about how cute he is. Don't think about the blood in the water behind you, the young man who didn't come back up to the surface. . . .*

We walked in silence. Ahead of me, Kerry had his arm around Patti. She kept shaking her head. I crossed my arms tightly in front of me to stop my shivering. Even Eric stayed silent, his eyes straight ahead of him as we followed Miguel up the path through the trees.

I felt relieved when I could see a bright circle of light up ahead. The trees ended, opening up into a wide, closely trimmed lawn. The lawn had been carefully raked. Not a leaf in sight. And beyond the lawn, the enormous mansion rose up, bathed in spotlights from the balconies above.

Another black-uniformed servant waited at the double front doors to greet us. Her nametag read: DELORES. She handed each of us a sealed white envelope as we filed into the front hall. "Don't open it until it's time," she kept repeating to everyone.

Time for what?

I blinked in the bright light of the entryway. A sparkling crystal chandelier hanging over our heads cast dazzling white light over us. The floor was black-and-white marble. The yellow wallpaper had beautiful white butterflies, hundreds of butterflies flying in perfect rows.

Miguel whispered something to Delores, then went running down a long hall. Delores looked troubled. Miguel must have told her about Randy's accident. But she forced a smile and led us to a wide, winding stairway at the side of the entrance.

"After the boat ride, you all probably want to go freshen up," Delores said. "We've opened some bedrooms upstairs for you to share. And you can drop off your coats and backpacks there."

"I'll share one with April," Eric said. He turned to her. "Don't beg. I already said I'd share one with you."

She grabbed the hood on his hoodie and tugged it down hard over his face.

"Is that a yes?" he asked.

We followed Delores up the stairs. We stepped out into a long, dimly lit hallway. Rooms on both sides all the way down to the end. As we followed her, we passed huge portraits on the walls, paintings of Fears, I guessed. Grim-looking people, sitting or standing stiffly against dark backgrounds. They didn't look evil, but they didn't look nice, either.

She motioned April, Geena, and me into the first bedroom. It was an enormous room with a king-sized bed against the far wall, covered in a satin navy blue bedspread. A tall mirror stretched behind a wide oak dresser. The room had its own bathroom. Twin lights suspended in cones from the ceiling sent a white light over the room.

"Is there a view?" I asked. I darted to the window and gazed out through the dirt-smeared glass. "All I can see are woods," I reported. "The trees come almost up to the house."

We tossed coats and backpacks onto the bed. I kept my tangerine jacket on. I'd freeze in just my camisole top. I'd packed a sweatshirt, but I didn't want to look sloppy.

Geena disappeared into the bathroom, carrying her cosmetics case. I glanced in the mirror behind the dresser. "Whoa!" My hair was standing out in all directions in big clumps. "The wind on the lake," I murmured, watching April's reflection in the mirror. "It looks like my hair is trying to escape my head."

She laughed. "You're funny, Rachel."

I pulled my hairbrush from my backpack and tried to tame my hair. Finally I gave up and put it up in a ponytail. When I turned to April, she was sitting on the edge of the bed, just staring blankly at the flowered wallpaper.

"What's wrong?"

She hesitated. "I was kind of like in a horror movie this week. For real," she said finally. She avoided my gaze.

"April, what are you talking about?" I crossed the room and sat down beside her.

She shook her head. "I was totally creeped out, Rachel. Seriously."

"By what? What happened to you?"

"A dead squirrel," April murmured. She finally turned to me. "It looked like it had been run over. I mean, it was squished flat in the middle."

I squinted at her, tapping the hairbrush against the palm of my hand. My mind was spinning. "I . . . don't understand."

"I . . . I got home after the basketball game. And I went to my room. And . . . I saw something under the sheets in my bed. It was a dead squirrel, stuffed under the covers."

"Omigod!" My cry escaped in a whisper.

April shivered. "My bedroom window was wide open. And someone . . . someone had stuffed a dead squirrel in my bed."

"Omigod! Omigod!" I slapped my hands against my cheeks. "No. No way. That's impossible." *I blamed Mac for the rat. I knew it had to be Mac. But . . .*

"Hey, what's wrong?" Geena strode out of the bathroom, zipping up her plastic cosmetics case.

"April found a dead squirrel in her bed," I said. "And I—"

"Noooo!" Geena screamed. The case fell from her hand and bounced on the carpet. "When? Friday night?"

April nodded.

"But—but—" Geena sputtered. "I don't believe it! Me, too! Not a squirrel. A baby raccoon. A dead baby raccoon. Under my covers. Squashed flat and its eyes were missing."

"Omigod! Omigod!" I struggled to get control. "I blamed Mac. I can't believe I blamed Mac."

"Blamed him for what?" Geena demanded.

"For the dead rat in my bed," I said.

They both gaped at me open-mouthed.

"You, too?" April whispered. "All three of us?"

"Roadkill," I muttered. I shook my head. "I blamed Mac."

Geena squinted at me. "Mac? Why Mac? Why would Mac put a dead animal in *my* bed?"

"He wouldn't," I said. "I must have gotten it all wrong. Mac wouldn't—"

"So who was it?" Geena asked.

I jumped to my feet, still gripping the hairbrush tightly. "Roadkill," I repeated. "Roadkill." My eyes went from Geena to April. "Someone was trying to warn us. Someone wanted to scare us *really bad*."

11.

AN AWESOME PARTY

We stared at each other. Someone had broken into our houses. Someone had carried a dead animal into our bedrooms and stuffed it under our blankets.

It was sick. Sick and gross.

"Does anyone have any idea who did it?" April asked.

Before anyone could answer, the door opened and Delores appeared. "Ready?" she asked. "I'll take you downstairs to the party room."

As we walked to the stairway, the two dark-haired dudes we didn't know led the way. Eric and Kerry tossed a white Nerf baseball back and forth. Spider dove to intercept it and almost fell down the stairs.

Patti hurried to keep up with us. I wanted to ask her if she received a road-kill gift, too. But as we reached the first floor, we were blasted by deafening guitar music that rang off the tile walls.

"Party time!" Eric shouted, pumping his hands over his head and doing a little dance.

Delores pushed open tall double doors, and we walked into an enormous room that looked like a movie set.

I blinked several times as I stared into the pulsing light. We were standing in what had to be a ballroom, with a high cathedral ceiling, lighted entirely by candlelight. Candles were hung in dark sconces along the walls. Two chandeliers decked with long candles hung low over our heads. Three walls held floor-to-ceiling bookshelves. A fire danced in a broad fireplace at the back wall.

For some crazy reason, I thought of the ballroom in the Beast's castle in that Disney movie Beth and I used to watch over and over, *Beauty and the Beast*.

Half in shadow, half in flickering orange light, Brendan stood in the center of the enormous room beside a long food table. He stepped forward with a big smile on his face, watching everyone's reaction to the incredible room. "Hey, guys," he called. "Welcome."

He wore a black V-necked sweater over a white T-shirt, charcoal-colored jeans, and red Converse sneakers. It was kind of his uniform. I liked it.

"I . . . uh . . . I just heard about the problem at the dock," he said, rubbing his chin. "Well, I want you to know it's been taken care of. Everything will be okay. And you're not stranded here, if you're worried about that. We've already sent for another pilot for the boat. And—"

"Is Randy okay?" April interrupted, shouting over the wailing guitars. The music poured from enormous twin speakers on the wall.

"Of course he is." Brendan replied. "Randy is feeling good. A little shaken. He lost a little blood. He might have a slight concussion. But don't worry about him. We're here to party—right?"

"Right!" The cry rang out over the music.

"Some of you haven't been to this house," Brendan said. "It's pretty awesome. You'll see. My great-great-grandparents built the house like a million years ago. And as we all know, my ancestors were all way weird."

"So are you!" Eric shouted.

That got a big laugh.

Brendan laughed, too. He scratched his head and squinted at Eric. "Did I invite you here? Really?"

"I only came for the beer," Eric shot back.

That got a big cheer. Some guys shouted, "Me, too!"

"No worries," Brendan said. "There's plenty of beer. Hey, I'm eighteen today. I'm legal in this state." He grinned. (Did I mention that I love the way his eyes crinkle up when he smiles?) "The rest of you are all eighteen, too—right?"

"Right!" everyone shouted. Kids pumped their fists in the air and cheered.

Brendan's expression changed. "I've always been blown

away by the stories about my weird ancestors," he said. "I've always wanted to have a party in this house they built. A party like back in the day, with all kinds of old-fashioned games."

"You mean like the original *Grand Theft Auto*?" one of the dark-haired boys called out. He was wearing a gray-and-white Benson School sweatshirt and black, straight-legged jeans.

Brendan gestured toward him. "Hey, any of you guys know my cousins? They don't go to Shadyside. They go to the Benson School." He pointed. "Morgan and Kenny Fear."

I studied them. They had the same dark hair and dark eyes and serious expressions as Brendan. They totally looked like Fears.

"Morgan is the tall skinny one," Brendan said. "Kenny is the fat slob."

Kenny jumped to his feet. "Hey, thanks—!"

"I had to invite them because they're family," Brendan said. "But I don't like them at all."

"We can't stand you, either," Morgan shot back. "You're a total jerk."

Kenny said, "We only came because our parents made us."

All three of them laughed. I could see they really *did* like each other a lot.

"You all can just ignore them," Brendan said. "They're totally antisocial, and they don't play well with others."

"Who can get along with *you*?" Morgan shouted.

"Do you still wet the bed?" Kenny asked.

"No. Kenny, *you're* the only one in the family who still does that," Brendan shot back. "Even when you're awake."

"Is this Family Fight Night?" Eric chimed in. "Are we supposed to vote on the *Biggest Loser*?"

"You win!" Kerry said, slapping Eric on the shoulder.

Lots of laughter rang off the high walls.

"Are we just going to stand here being nice to each other all night?" Eric complained.

"I've got some things planned," Brendan said, turning serious. "Some games and things. But we can do that later. I mean, we have all night—right? First, let's chow down and *get TRASHED*."

I followed Kerry and Patti to the long dining table. It was covered in a beautiful burgundy cloth—and seemed like the whole table was filled with silver platters and beautiful china.

"No way!" I cried. "There's enough food here for a hundred people!"

I saw three different kinds of pizzas and a platter stacked high with cheeseburgers and big bowls of salad. Four servers dressed in black uniforms stood ready to help behind the table. One of them held a silver knife and began to carve a giant ham and a whole roast beef. Moving down the table, I saw a huge casserole filled with macaroni and cheese. Another platter was piled high with French fries. And if that wasn't enough I saw a huge bowl of mashed potatoes, bread and rolls, a pile of shrimp and crab legs, breads, cheeses. It was an amazing feast.

A table beside it had been set up as a bar. A black-uniformed bartender was helping kids to sodas and beer in tall slender glasses.

This is insane, I thought. There were only ten of us here . . . eleven with Brendan. . . . *Is this how Brendan's family lives all the time?*

Everyone began piling dinner plates high with food. I turned and gazed around at the amazing room. It really was like standing in a ballroom from the nineteenth century. The candlelight made it magical, shadowy, and special. I really did feel as if I was in a Disney castle.

"Earth to Rachel," a voice said.

I turned and saw Brendan smiling at me. He had two glasses of beer in his hands. He handed one to me. "You looked like you were off in space somewhere."

"No . . . I was just gazing around," I stammered. "I mean, this room . . ."

He shook his head. "My parents are crazy. See all those books on the shelves? They bought them by the yard. Do you believe it? 'I'll take four hundred yards of books, please.'"

"Weird," I said.

He tipped his glass against mine as if toasting. We both took a long sip of beer. "Glad you could come," he said. His eyes locked on mine.

"Me, too."

"This is the most awesome room," he said. "But parts of this house are like out of a Frankenstein movie. No joke. There's even a room downstairs that's like a dungeon. Really. You'd swear it was a torture chamber."

"Sweet," I said.

That made him laugh. "Are you into torture?"

"Seriously," I said. "My house doesn't have a basement. Otherwise, I'd definitely have a torture chamber."

He nodded. He kept his eyes on mine. He didn't blink. "Where do you live?"

"On Knobb Road. A few blocks from Lefty's. It's a tiny house." I gestured with both hands. "Actually, my house would fit in this room."

He took another long sip of beer. It left a line of foam on his upper lip. I had this crazy urge to lick it off.

Whoa. Stay cool, Rachel.

"A few years ago, we had a bigger house on Park Drive," I said. "But . . . uh . . . things changed for my dad, and we had to move."

Bor-ing. Rachel, he's going to fall asleep listening to you.

He wiped the foam off his mouth. Then he brushed a hand through his wavy, dark hair. "I really wanted you to come. I hope you have a good time. Maybe later, you and I . . ." His voice trailed off.

He's actually flirting with me. "This is an awesome party," I said.

A sly smile crossed his face. A *teasing* smile. "Rachel, you're not *scared* to be here, are you?"

"Scared?" I laughed. "Why would I be scared?"

He leaned close. "I have some things planned."

He stayed like that for a moment, with his face close to mine. I actually thought he wanted to kiss me. It was one of those moments where time stopped, like when you pause a movie and everyone freezes in place.

I wanted to kiss him. I moved my face closer. But then his cousin Kenny came up and bumped Brendan from behind, and Brendan spun around to talk to him.

I let out a long breath. *Don't rush things, Rachel.*

A wave of happiness rushed over me. I suddenly felt all fluttery. Here I was in this amazing mansion, with the coolest group of kids in school, no parents around, amazing food, and all the beer you could drink. And a guy I'd had a crush on for years was actually flirting with me.

Best day ever?

The boat pilot, Randy, flashed into my mind. I pictured him again, hitting his head on the dock piling and sinking into the water. And again I thought about Geena and April finding dead animals in their beds, just like me.

I shook my head, as if shaking those thoughts away.

Nothing is going to spoil this day. Nothing is going to keep me from having an awesome time at this party.

The rock music ended. Dance music began to pound from the speakers. Some kids were still stuffing their faces. But a few got up to dance, beer glasses in one hand.

I took another sip of beer and wandered over to the food table. Patti and Kerry were being served seconds—slices of pepperoni pizza—by one of the waiters, and I lined up behind them.

We stood against a bookshelf, eating our pizza slices. "I've been here before," Kerry said. "I still don't believe this room. You could have a full basketball court here. Seriously."

I laughed. "Is basketball all you think about?"

"No. I think about Patti, too." He wrapped his free hand around her waist from behind and nuzzled his face in the back of her hair.

"How come you tell everyone you're just friends?" I said, shouting over the thumping music.

Patti shrugged. "Why not? It's a little joke we have. To confuse people. We're friends. We're just *very close* friends."

They both laughed.

Still holding onto Patti, Kerry said something else, but I couldn't hear him over the music. He and Patti laughed.

I laughed, too, pretending I'd heard him. I finished my

pizza and returned the plate to the food table. I asked, and one of the waiters pointed the way to the bathroom, through a glass door at the far end of the ballroom. As I crossed the room, I saw Brendan watching me from the middle of a circle of girls.

Sweet.

The hall leading to the bathroom was dimly lit, the carpet ragged. More dark oil portraits of Fears stared at me from the walls on both sides.

I turned the corner, following the waiter's directions. He said the restroom would be halfway down the hall on the right. Even this far from the ballroom, I could still hear the *boom boom boom* of the drumbeat from the pounding dance music.

I took a few steps—then stopped when I heard a hoarse cry. At first, I wasn't sure if I'd really heard it or not. I thought it might be part of the music drifting down the hall.

I took a few more steps and heard the cry more clearly.

"Help me! Is anyone there? Please—help me!"

A young man's voice. Randy, the boat pilot? Yes. It sounded like him.

My breath caught in my throat. I heard him again, a muffled voice from somewhere nearby.

"Can anyone hear me? Help me! *Please*—somebody."

I forced myself to breathe again and lurched toward the sound of the cries.

"Oh." I let out a soft cry as two black-uniformed servants stepped in front of me.

They eyed me suspiciously. I recognized Antonio instantly. The other one was tall and broad-shouldered, big like a football player, with curly blond hair. He had a cigarette dangling from his lips. "Can I help you?" he asked.

"I . . . heard the shouts," I said. "It sounded like Randy. The boat pilot. Like he was calling for help."

"I didn't hear anything," the server said. He turned to Antonio. "Did you hear anything?"

Antonio shook his head. "No. I didn't hear anything. Are you looking for the ladies' room?"

"Yes," I said. "But I heard someone. Really. He was calling for help. He . . . he sounded so frightened."

"We'll check into it," Antonio said.

"Yeah. Right away," his partner added.

They stood side by side, blocking my path. Antonio pointed. "The ladies' room—it's right down there. On the right. You can't miss it."

"But—but—" I sputtered.

"We're on it. Really. No worries," Antonio said.

I could see there was no point arguing with them. I turned and started to walk away. I was halfway down the hall when I heard Antonio's shout:

"Enjoy the party. Have a good one."

12.

GHOST STORIES

The dance music was still pumping when I returned to the party room. I saw Eric dancing with April. He was going berserk, jerking his body around like a spastic robot, and she was standing there watching him, her hand to her mouth, obviously embarrassed.

Eric, of course, *cannot* be embarrassed.

April is shy and quiet. Eric isn't her type at all. I wondered how he was able to drag her onto the dance floor. He probably *did* drag her.

Morgan and Kenny, Brendan's cousins, were slouched in a corner by themselves in their matching Benson School sweatshirts, beer glasses in their hands. I felt bad. They didn't know anyone here, and they seemed totally uncomfortable. Morgan kept glancing at his phone, then shoving it back in his pocket.

Maybe Brendan wasn't kidding about them. Maybe they really *were* antisocial.

I searched for Brendan. I was desperate to tell him about Randy's cries for help and the two servers who had no intention of helping him. But I didn't have a chance. The music cut off abruptly, and Brendan stood at the front of the room, waving his arms above his head to get everyone's attention.

It took a while for everyone to get quiet. Someone had spilled a plate of macaroni and cheese on the floor, and a waiter stooped to clean it up. Eric was still doing his insane dance moves even though the music had stopped.

It was a little bit funny, but he wasn't impressing April. She had already crept away from him, shaking her head, her hands balled into tight fists. He was so clueless, he didn't even realize she had left.

"I want to start," Brendan said. "You know. Get things rolling."

We gathered in a tight group in front of him. Only his cousins held back, murmuring to themselves, not smiling.

Brendan rubbed his hands together and flashed us a mad-scientist, gleeful grin. "My devious mind has a lot of ideas for tonight," he said. "I've planned some awesome games."

"Stop him! He's a crazy Fear!" Eric shouted. "We're all going to DIE!"

I laughed and so did a few other kids.

Brendan rolled his eyes. "Why do I put up with you?"

"Because I'm an awesome dude?" Eric answered.

"No," Brendan said. "That's not it."

"Because you feel sorry for him?" Spider Webb shouted.

"Yes," Brendan said. "You got it." He waited for everyone to stop laughing. Eric laughed, too. Eric is obnoxious but there's something lovable about him, too. I'd always wondered if it was possible to have a serious conversation with Eric. I'd never seen him be serious, even in school. *Especially* in school.

"We're going to start with a real old game from back in the day," Brendan announced. "Later, I'm going to tell you about a game I've been developing. I've been working hard on it, and I think it's way cool."

A waiter walked down the line of kids with a tray of beer glasses. Brendan took a glass off the tray and drank half of it down. "The first game is old," he said, licking his lips. "Like it goes back to the nineteenth century. A scavenger hunt."

A few kids groaned.

"I thought we were going to play Spin the Bottle," Eric said.

"Yes, you should let Eric play Spin the Bottle," Kerry shouted to Brendan. "It's the only way he'll ever get a girl to kiss him."

More laughter.

"Not funny," Eric muttered.

Brendan waved everyone quiet. "I know, I know. You all probably think a scavenger hunt is a game for kids. But not in this old house. Once you leave this ballroom, you're in a different world. You'll find miles of dark, twisting hallways on all the floors. Some of the rooms haven't been opened for years. Some of the rooms have mysterious objects, masks, figures . . . weird things we can't even recognize.

"My ancestors were strange. Everyone knows that. And over the years, their interests and hobbies caused them to collect many things most people have never seen. Maybe there are things you won't *want* to see."

"*Oooowooooo.*" Kerry did a ghostlike howl.

"Call the Ghost Hunters."

"Brendan is trying to scare us."

"Next he'll tell us the house is haunted," Patti said.

"The house *is* haunted," Brendan said. "Do you really think an old mansion like this doesn't have its ghosts? My dad said when he was a teenager, he took his girlfriend up to the attic, and they both saw a ghost. The room suddenly turned cold as ice. And he and his girlfriend saw someone in the doorway.

"It was a young woman in a long, old-fashioned dress, like from the 1800s. She was all silver, glowing in a silvery light. Like it was shining out of her, so bright my dad said he had to look away. And when he turned back, she was gone. Dad said he was badly shaken. It was too bold and too real. He never went up to the attic again."

Silence for a moment.

Then Eric murmured, "Good one, Brendan."

That got a pretty big laugh from everyone. "Eric," Brendan said, "maybe you'd like to *start* in the attic."

Eric stuck his chin out. "Dare me? Do you? Dare me to start in the attic? Your dad's fake ghost story doesn't scare me, dude."

Brendan frowned at him. "Fake ghost story? Eric, you know my father. Oliver Fear. The most serious man on earth. I don't think he has ever cracked a joke. I don't even think he ever *laughed* at a joke. And believe me, he never made up a story in his life. If he says he saw a ghost in the attic . . ."

"We're all shivering and shaking," Eric said. He did a wild shimmy, shivering and shaking his whole body.

"Eric, I'll come with you." Delia Rodgers spoke up. "To the attic. I'm desperate to see a ghost."

Eric's eyes went wide. "Seriously?" Delia had never paid any attention to him before.

She tugged at a strand of her white-blonde hair. "I watch *Ghost Hunters* every week," she said. "It's my favorite show."

"Maybe you'll see ghosts on your scavenger hunt," Brendan said. "This is the Fear family, after all. I know you all know the stories. We're evil."

"Speak for yourself," Morgan chimed in.

"Brendan is the *most* evil," cousin Kenny said.

Brendan ignored them. He held up a white envelope.

"You all were given these envelopes at the door. Take them out now. This is your list of the things you need to find for the scavenger hunt."

I tore open my envelope and gazed down the list of objects:

A bird skeleton
A jar of silver bullets
A mummy's finger
A black flower
A stuffed rabbit
A live tarantula
Raven feathers
A silver urn filled with ashes

Totally weird.

"You'll have to do a lot of exploring," Brendan said over the muttered conversations around the room. "The objects you need to find have been hidden all over the house. And I have to apologize that a lot of the rooms and halls are dark. This is a summer house, and some of the generators have been turned off. Of course, finding things in the dark is more fun—right?"

"Do you really have a mummy's finger in this house?" April asked.

Brendan nodded. "Doesn't every house have a mummy's finger?"

"Hey, how come Geena's name is at the bottom of my list?" Eric demanded. "You mean I have to find Geena?"

"Eric, you're at the bottom of *my* list," Geena said, waving her piece of paper in front of him.

"That's because you're partners," Brendan said. "We're going to divide into twos. Your partner's name is at the bottom of the page."

"You mean I have to go into a dark room with Eric?" Geena cried.

Patti pointed to Spider at the end of the line of kids. I guessed she and Spider were going to be partners. Could she stand to be separated from Kerry for an hour or more?

"Hey, Kenny and I are partners?" cousin Morgan said.

"No one else could stand to be with you," Brendan said.

"I can't stand to be with him, either," Kenny said.

They gave each other playful shoves.

"Your cousins are cute," Delia said to Brendan. "If you shut your eyes."

Laughter all around.

I raised my list and gazed at the name at the bottom of the page:

Brendan.

Brendan wanted me to be his partner.

I knew this was an awesome party!

Eric bumped up next to me. "Rachel, who's your partner? Want to trade with Geena? Geena doesn't like me. You and I—?"

"I don't think so," I said. "Brendan is my partner."

Eric's eyes went wide. He shouted: "Hey, Brendan—no fair. You can't be in the game. You know where everything is hidden."

"No, I don't," Brendan said. "I didn't hide the objects. Some of the workers hid everything before you all arrived. I'm like you. I'm clueless. Really. I don't know where anything is."

Some kids grumbled about that. "Brendan, who's your partner?" Spider called.

"Rachel," Brendan said.

"Ooh, Brendan—are you going to take Rachel up to the attic?" Delia said.

That got a pretty good laugh. I could feel myself blushing. "No. I'm taking *Brendan* to the attic," I said. It was a lame joke. But it made Brendan smile.

"Okay, partner up, guys. We'll meet back here in two hours," Brendan said. "The team that collects the most items wins. If anyone gets lost, just scream for help. Probably, no one will hear you. But it'll make you feel better."

He started toward me, but Kerry stepped in his way. "Brendan, a live tarantula?" Kerry said, waving his list. "How are Delia and I supposed to bring it back here? In our hands?"

"It's just a baby," Brendan said. "It's in a glass cage."

Eric and Geena were huddled together, going over their list. "This stuff is hidden on all the floors?" Geena asked.

"Everywhere but the basement," Brendan said. "The basement is filled with summer stuff. So we can't use it."

"Wait! Before we start, Brendan, can I ask you a question?" April said. All eyes turned to her. She held her scavenger hunt list in one hand. "Do you have dead squirrels on the list?"

Brendan squinted at her. "Excuse me?"

"Dead squirrels," April repeated. "Because I had one at home. A dead squirrel in my bed. Was that part of your game?"

Brendan's mouth had dropped open. "I don't know what you're talking about, April. Why would there be a dead squirrel?"

"I had a dead raccoon," Geena said.

"Me, too!" Patti cried before I had a chance to chime in.

"Did everyone coming to this party get a dead animal?" April demanded.

Brendan was blinking rapidly, his face all tight, as if he was struggling to understand.

"I didn't get a dead animal," Kerry said.

"Neither did I," Eric and Spider said in unison.

"I . . . I don't know anything about this," Brendan said finally. "I can't believe it. Really. Do you think . . . ? Do you think someone was trying to ruin my party? I mean . . . someone wanted you to *blame* me for putting them there?"

"Are you telling us the truth?" Patti demanded.

"Of course I didn't do it," Brendan replied. "No way. That's horrible. Where would I get dead animals? Do you think I collect them or something? How would I get them into your houses?"

Everyone started talking at once.

"Why would I do that?" Brendan shouted over the voices. "Why would I do a thing like that right before my party? I . . . I can't believe someone did that to you."

But then his expression changed. He seemed to freeze. His eyes went wide, and he made a gurgling sound.

"Brendan? Are you okay?" I called. "Are you *choking*?"

"Omigod," he murmured. "It can't be. It *can't* be."

The room grew quiet again. Brendan's hands were shaking. He grabbed the edge of the food table to steady himself. "Great-Aunt Victoria," he said, his voice cracking.

We drew closer. I could barely hear him.

"Did I ever tell any of you about my father's great-aunt Victoria?"

No one replied. Eric flashed me a look, like: *What's up with Brendan?*

Brendan picked up a bottle of water and took a long swallow. Then he turned back to us.

"My dad told us the story. You see, Victoria Fear inherited this house a long time ago. I don't know exactly when. Dad said she was a very weird person. She didn't like other people. She didn't get along with anyone. She lived here alone for many years."

Brendan finished the water in the bottle and tossed the bottle to the floor. "Victoria had only one thing in life that she enjoyed. It was taxidermy. You know. Stuffing animals after they died. She collected *hundreds* of animals. No exaggeration. Hundreds. And she spent all her time in her taxidermy room, stuffing animals, putting them back together, mounting them. And—"

"What does this have to do with what happened to us?" April interrupted.

"I'm getting to it," Brendan replied. "This is the weird part. Sometimes other members of the Fear family would come to the house to visit. This was supposed to be a summer house for the whole family. But Victoria never wanted to share it with anyone. And many times, my dad told me, visitors would find a dead animal under the sheets of their bed. It was crazy Victoria's way of telling them they weren't welcome."

April opened her mouth to say something, but stopped. No one spoke.

Brendan tapped his hand tensely against the tabletop. "You probably don't believe in ghosts," he said. "But if you were a member of my family, you would believe. And I know it's totally insane, but I really think—"

Eric spoke up. "You think the ghost of Victoria Fear

put dead animals in their beds to tell us to stay away from this house? Do you also believe that fairies and elves have a midnight dance in the woods under the full moon?"

Brendan shrugged. "I know what it sounds like. But you have to remember about my family . . . About this house."

"Give us a break, Brendan," Geena said, shaking her head. "*You* put the roadkill in our beds. So we'd all be scared and get in the mood for your scary party."

"No way!" Brendan cried. "That's sick. I wouldn't do anything like that. How *could* I? When? When could I do it? I was at the Tigers' game. Isn't that right, Kerry? You saw me at the game—right?"

Kerry nodded. "Yeah. I saw you there. About halfway up the bleachers."

"I just want to have a fun party," Brendan said. "I don't want to scare anyone. You don't have to believe in ghosts. But you have to believe me. I didn't do it. Maybe someone else was out to scare you, someone who didn't want you to come to Fear Island."

He paused for a moment. "Just let me tell you the rest of the story," he said finally. "No one knows how or when Victoria Fear died. But my dad said that one summer, probably in the 1920s, a distant relative named Dennis Fear came to this house to see Victoria. No one answered the door. He stepped inside and found room after room cluttered with stuffed animals. *Real* animals.

"He searched the house for Victoria. And in a bedroom upstairs he found her. She was standing in front of a fireplace, eyes glowing. He called to her, but she didn't move. Dennis walked over to her and discovered the most horrifying thing he'd ever see in his lifetime.

"Victoria had been stuffed. The job was perfect. She looked totally lifelike. Dennis couldn't believe it. His eyes moved from her face down. And then he saw the long needle in her hand. And he started to scream—because he realized that *Victoria Fear had stuffed HERSELF.*"

13.

"WORRY MUCH?"

I lingered behind as the teams headed out of the ball-room, holding their scavenger hunt lists, talking mostly about Victoria Fear. Brendan walked over to me. "Ready?"

"For sure," I said. "So, you like to tell ghost stories?"

He didn't smile. "My family has enough of them," he said softly.

I narrowed my eyes at him. "You didn't make that story up?"

"I don't have to make them up," he answered. "Trust me. Let's go. We don't want to give everyone else a head start."

I raised the list. "You really don't know where anything is?"

He raised his right hand. "I swear. Let's start on the third floor."

"Why?"

"Because it hasn't been used in a lot of years, and it's filled with rows of empty bedrooms. Perfect places for hiding stuff."

He put his hand on my back and led me to the ball-room door. "It'll be pretty dark up there. You're not afraid of the dark, are you?"

"Terrified," I said. I gazed into his eyes. "Why do you keep asking me if I'm scared?"

He shrugged. "No reason."

"I don't scare easy," I said.

He smiled. "We'll see." He held open the door for me, and we stepped out of the ballroom. I could hear kids down the hall. Some chose to start on the first floor. Others were climbing the broad stairway at the front entry hall.

"We'll take a shortcut," Brendan said. He led the way down the hall toward the back of the house.

"This isn't fair," I said. "You know the house better than anyone."

He grinned. "Don't worry about it, Rachel. You want to *win*—don't you?"

Pale gray evening light filtered in from a tall, dust-smeared window at the far end. We passed the enormous kitchen with stacks of dirty plates and cups on a long counter. Warm air floated out from the kitchen, carrying the tangy aroma of the pizzas that had been baked there.

"I . . . I have to tell you something," I said. "I was walking down the other hall, and I heard something. It was Randy, I'm pretty sure. And he was calling for help. I tried to go see him. But these two workers stopped me and—"

Brendan squeezed the back of my neck. A gentle squeeze, but it startled me "Worry much?" he said.

"Well, the workers blocked my path and—"

"Randy is fine," Brendan said. "Antonio told me he's totally okay. He'll have a bump on his head, but he will be fine. Come on. Follow me. We have a game to win!"

I stared hard at him. I wanted to believe him. But how could I be sure that he was telling the truth?

We started walking again. The hall made a sharp turn to the right. The carpet ended and our shoes clicked on dark hardwood floors.

Brendan stopped and turned to the wall. I saw a door with a small round window in the center. He pushed a black button on the wall, and the door slid open.

"An elevator!" I cried. "You have an elevator in your house?"

He nodded and motioned for me to step inside. A small bulb in the ceiling sent a cone of orange light over us. The elevator was tiny. Maybe three or four people could squeeze in.

"My grandfather had it put in," Brendan said. "In her

last years, my grandmother was in a wheelchair. She couldn't use the stairs. So he would take her up to her room in this elevator." He grinned. "*Every* house should have an elevator, right?"

"Not mine," I said. "It's only one floor."

He laughed. "Well, your elevator could go *sideways*."

The door slid closed. He pushed a lever, and the car started to rise. It made a loud hum. We moved very slowly. The ceiling light flickered.

Brendan kept his eyes on the window. I saw a flash of light as we passed the second floor. *He's so cute,* I thought. And then, without thinking, I blurted out: "How come you invited me to your party?"

He spun around.

"I mean . . . we're in some classes together," I said. "But we're not friends. I mean . . . I was glad, but . . ."

Please. Let me just swallow my tongue and choke to death on the elevator floor. How stupid am I?

Brendan didn't seem to notice how embarrassed I was.

It wasn't the first time I blurted out what I was thinking. Such a bad habit.

"I saw you hanging with Amy a lot," he said.

"Yeah. She's my best friend," I said. "You don't know her very well, do you?"

He frowned. "No. I don't. We've never been in the same classes and—"

I didn't hear the rest of Brendan's sentence, I shrieked as the elevator jolted. The light went out. The car stopped. I blinked into the total darkness. It was so dark, I couldn't see Brendan even though he was right next to me.

"Stalled," he said calmly. "Stalled between floors."

"Can you . . . d-do something?" I stammered.

"It hasn't been used in a long time. I should have tested it."

"But, Brendan—"

My eyes slowly adjusted to the darkness. I watched him work the control lever back and forth. The car didn't budge.

"Is there an alarm?" I asked. "Can we call someone to help us?"

"No. No alarm."

My heart started to pound. I could feel the blood pulsing at my temples. Sometimes I get really claustrophobic. "Well . . . is there enough air to breathe?"

"Probably. But it's already stuffy in here, isn't it."

"People will notice. They'll miss us. They'll search for us."

"Eventually," Brendan said.

I stood there, silent for a moment, trying to force my heartbeats to slow down. Brendan turned to me. He slid his hands around my waist. Again, I thought he was going to kiss me.

And he did. Gently at first, then with more feeling.

His lips moved over mine. He shut his eyes. At first, I was hesitant. But then I kissed him back. So intense. I didn't want it to end.

Finally, he lifted his head and whispered, "That was nice."

My heart was suddenly pounding. I could still feel the warmth of his lips on mine.

"But . . . the elevator—?" I said finally.

He grinned. "The elevator is fine. I just wanted to kiss you."

"I . . . I don't *believe* you!" I cried. But the truth is, I was thrilled. "You scared me nearly to death just for a kiss?"

He shrugged. "Pretty much. Couldn't help myself," he said.

I struggled to read his expression, half-smiling, half-studying me.

He turned and shoved the control lever. The ceiling light flickered on, and the car jerked, then began to rise again.

"I don't think you'll be a good partner if you just want to flirt with me," I teased.

"I'll be a good partner," he said. He squeezed my shoulder. "I promise."

The door slid open, and I followed him into the third

floor hallway. The air was hot up here, and it smelled sour, like old clothes. Again, the only light came from the darkening gray sky through a tall window at the end of the hall.

"I'll try the hall lights," Brendan said. He flipped a switch on the wall. Then flipped it several times. "No. No lights. The generator must be off."

I squinted at him. "This is another joke, right?"

"I wish."

I gazed down the hall. It seemed to stretch on forever in a straight line with rooms on both sides. I couldn't see the end of the hall. Too dark.

The floor creaked under the thin carpet as we began to walk toward the first doorway. We were the only ones on this floor. The other guys were still exploring downstairs.

"I forgot about flashlights," Brendan said. "I should have passed them out to everyone."

I heard a fluttering sound from down the hall. Like curtains flapping in the wind? I followed Brendan into a small bedroom. At least, I *thought* it was a bedroom from the size. There was no bed or dresser. No furniture at all. Cartons were stacked in tall towers against one wall.

"Some of these rooms haven't been used in years," Brendan said. He tugged the cord of a window blind and let some gray evening light wash into the room. "Rachel, do you have your list?"

"Yeah." I pulled it out of my pocket.

Brendan was on his knees behind a tower of cartons. "Check this out."

I stepped up behind him and gazed at the object he was holding. A gigantic egg.

"It's an ostrich egg," he said. "Is it on the list?"

I raised the paper and gazed down the list. "No. No ostrich egg."

"Too bad." He set the big egg down on the floor. He pointed. "See if there's anything in that closet. Then meet me in the next room."

I edged through two stacks of boxes and stepped up to the closet. I grabbed the knob, twisted it, and tugged. The door didn't budge. I tried again. Twisted the knob the other direction and gave a hard pull.

The door flew open. Startled, I stumbled backward. I caught my balance and stared into the closet. Empty. I took a few steps closer. I saw three shelves, all empty. The floor was coated with a thick carpet of white dust.

"Nothing here," I said, then realized Brendan wasn't there. I pushed the closet door shut and stepped out of the room. "Brendan?" My voice sounded hollow in the long narrow hallway.

I heard the flapping sound again. I squinted into the gray light. Couldn't see anything. I stepped into the room across the hall. "Hey, Brendan?" No. The room was dark and empty.

"Brendan? Where are you?" I shouted.

No reply.

I heard the flapping again, and a high, shrill chittering sound. Mice? No. Mice don't flap.

I poked my head into the next room. "Brendan? Are you here?"

Silence. In the shadowy light, I could make out a long couch and two side tables. A desk against one wall. Some kind of office. But no Brendan.

"Hey," I shouted. "Brendan? Where *are* you?"

I heard the fluttering sound, closer now. And the shrill *eeeeeeeee.*

And squinting into the blackness, I saw tiny red lights. No. Not lights. Tiny red *eyes*.

"Oh, no," I whispered. A chill of fear tightened the back of my neck.

I stared at the sets of tiny red eyes at the far end of the hall, glowing bright as car taillights. Fluttering wings and glowing red eyes. It took me so long to realize they were bats.

A huge nest of bats. And I was disturbing them, invading their territory. I realized I was holding my breath. I let it out in a long, shuddering *whoosh*.

"Brendan, there are bats up here!" I whispered. "Can you hear me?"

Silence.

"Where *are* you? Brendan?"

I screamed as I felt a burst of hot air above my head. The bat flew over me before I realized what was happening.

And then I covered my face as the fluttering, squealing bats came swooping through the hall, red eyes sparkling with fury.

14.

HANGED

I dropped to my knees and covered my head with both arms. I could feel the puffs of wind off their wings as they darted over me.

A bat bumped my shoulder. I screamed. It bounced off me and hit the wall. Then it scrambled back up into the air.

At least a dozen bats flew past. I didn't wait for them to come soaring back. I jumped to my feet and started to run. My shoes kept catching in the ragged, worn carpet. I hurtled through the darkness, my heart pounding, past endless dark rooms.

"Brendan? Hey—Brendan?" I choked out his name.

I could hear the chittering of the bats behind me. Were they preparing to swoop at me again?

I reached the far wall and stopped. I struggled to catch my breath. Where were the stairs going down? Shouldn't there be stairs here?

I leaned against the wall and waited for my heart to stop leaping around in my chest. Held my breath and got it together. *Yes.* I forced back my panic.

Rachel, take a deep breath and calm down, I told myself. *You can make it back to the elevator. So what if it's dark up here? What's the big deal about darkness? Ignore the bats. Walk back to the elevator and go downstairs. No biggie.*

Before Beth went off to college, she and I used to watch the most disgusting horror movies we could find on Netflix every weekend. And *Beth* was always the one who got scared.

Not me. Not me. I'm not the scared one.

I suddenly remembered the day our parents took us to the Waynesville zoo. Funny how things pop up in your mind. You have no control over your memories.

We were in a House of Darkness, a building with tall glass cases of nocturnal animals. Beth and I pressed up against the glass to see the bats in one case. Suddenly, the bats went berserk, flying crazily in all directions. Bats shot into the glass, flapping frantically against it, batting the cage front with their mouse bodies, banging hard again and again, right in our faces, as if trying to get at us.

Beth started to shriek. She spread her hands over her eyes and screamed. I had to make her stop. I had to calm her down. I took her by the shoulders and led her away from the bat cage.

Later, she said she was pretending to be in a horror

movie, like the ones we watched every weekend. But I knew the truth. I knew she had freaked. Lost it. Totally lost it. And I knew I was the grown-up, at least in that situation.

I am the grown-up now. I can handle anything.

I took another few seconds to get myself together. I wanted to scream for Brendan again. But I was afraid my shouts would alarm the bats, make them come swooping back at me.

I stared into the darkness to the other end of the hall. I couldn't hear them now. They were silent. But I could see the tiny red dots of their eyes staring back at me.

The elevator seemed a mile away. I decided if I walked slowly, carefully, silently, maybe I wouldn't disturb the bats. I forced myself away from the wall and started walking, almost on tiptoe, trying not to make a sound.

But the floorboards beneath the thin carpet squeaked with every footstep, and I could see the red eyes flash, suddenly alert. The shrill chittering started up again, as if the bats were sounding the alarm.

I stopped. I could see the dark, round window of the elevator just a few yards away. If only I could get there and jump inside it before the bats decided to attack again.

Bats don't attack people. That's what we learned in our Earth Sciences class last year. *Bats don't attack people—unless provoked.*

What did that mean exactly?

I think I was provoking them by being in the hall. Invading their space.

I took a step. Then another. I kept my eyes on the elevator door. I forced myself not to look at the bats.

I stopped in front of the door. The window was black. I squinted in the darkness, searching for the button on the wall. My hand shook as I raised it and pushed the button.

I thought maybe the elevator was still on this floor, and the door would slide open for me. But no. Nothing happened.

I listened for the hum of the car, but I couldn't hear anything over the shrill chirp and whistle of the bats. I pressed the button again. Again.

Come on. Come on!

I pushed my face against the glass of the elevator window. I struggled to hear. No. Nothing happening. Was the car stuck on another floor? Was the elevator turned off?

The bats' cries grew more shrill. They rang in my ears like a dozen ambulance sirens, all wailing at once. I heard the flap and flutter of their wings again.

The back of my neck prickled. I imagined their tiny bat claws hanging on me, digging into my skin. Imagined the sharp bite of their little pointed teeth.

"No!" I slammed my fist against the elevator door.

"Where *are* you?" I screamed. I was losing it, but I didn't care.

I spun away, breathing hard. Okay. No elevator. That meant I had to find the stairway. There had to be a stairway down to the second floor.

Swinging away from the bats, I lurched toward the other end of the hall. Dark doorways whirred past me in a blur.

I stopped when I saw a square of dim light spilling onto the carpet from an open doorway. Was someone in there? Was Brendan in there?

"Brendan?"

I started to jog. Stepped into the square of light. Turned into the doorway.

Squinted into the gray light, gray as a fog. And screamed.

Screamed as I saw the body. A boy's body. A boy in a black sweater and gray jeans. Hanged. His neck tilted, head slanting at a horrible angle. The boy hanging from a rope that stretched down from a high ceiling rafter.

"Oh, no. Oh, no."

The body swung slowly around—and I stared at Brendan's pale face, eyes frozen wide open.

Brendan, hanged from the ceiling.

I tried to look away, but my eyes stopped on something on the floor. A sheet of white paper beneath Brendan's shoes. White paper with writing on it. Some kind of note?

Staggering forward, almost against my will, I moved close enough to gaze down at the carefully printed words on the paper:

ANYONE FOR A GAME OF HANGMAN?

15.

"SOMEONE IS THREATENING ME"

I stared at the words until they became a blur.

And then I uttered a choked cry as hands gripped my shoulders hard from behind. I stumbled off-balance as someone pulled me back. Forced me to the doorway.

"Hey—!" I found my voice and cried out. I spun around. "Brendan!"

"Rachel, here you are. I heard you scream, but I couldn't find you." He let go of my shoulders. His dark eyes were wide, his face twisted in a confused frown.

"Brendan, I thought—"

He took a step back and stared over my shoulder at the figure swinging from the rope.

"It—it's a mannequin," I stammered. "The light was so weird. It was so hard to see. Brendan, I thought it was *you*."

He didn't reply. He pushed past me and stepped up to the mannequin. He picked the note up from the floor. I could see his eyes reading it again and again.

"Brendan—are you okay?"

Finally, he turned to me. "It looks like me. It's even wearing my clothes."

"I know," I said, stepping up to him. "I thought—"

He crinkled the note into a ball and tossed it across the room. "Who did this?" he muttered in a low voice. "Who would do this? Is someone trying to ruin my party?"

"It's got to be a joke," I said. "Maybe—"

He exploded. "A joke? Seriously? A joke?"

I was startled by his sudden anger. But as I stared at his face, I could see the anger turn to fear.

"Not a joke," he murmured, shaking his head. The pink circles on his cheeks had darkened to red.

"It's a threat, Rachel. Someone is threatening me." He grabbed the mannequin, gave it a hard push, and watched it swing back and forth. "First the dead animals in the beds. Then this. This is a definite warning."

"Wait. Think about it," I said, grabbing his arm. "It could just be a sick joke. Maybe Eric . . . ?"

"Eric?" he said. He shook his head. "No. Eric is a joker, but this isn't his style. Eric is a goof. He's never mean." He raised his eyes to me. "No way. Not Eric. We're good friends. He wouldn't do this."

"What are you going to do?" I asked. "Stop the scavenger hunt? Send everyone home?"

He turned and narrowed his eyes at me. "No way," he

said. "I planned this party for weeks. I'm not going to let anyone spoil it."

"But if you think this is a serious threat—" I started.

"I don't care. I'm not stopping the scavenger hunt. I'm not stopping the party."

"But, Brendan, don't you think you should call everyone together? Maybe tell everyone what happened up here? If it *is* just a joke, you don't want—"

"If it *is* a joke, it's a pretty hostile one," he said. "Look at this thing." He shoved the mannequin again and sent it swinging. "Hanging someone is not a funny joke."

"If you think it's a real threat, you should definitely phone the police," I said. "Seriously."

"Phone the police? How? The phones are shut off. And cell phones don't work here."

He pounded both fists against the mannequin and sent it swinging again. "Who would do this? Let's think. Let's think."

I knew he wasn't talking to me. He was talking to himself.

Brendan shook his head and began to pace back and forth, avoiding the dummy, which twirled slowly on its rope. "My cousins? Morgan and Kenny have a sick sense of humor. Those two guys are pretty dark. Probably because they're Fears." He stopped pacing and gazed at the dust-smeared window, obviously thinking hard.

"But when could they do this?" I asked. "Your cousins

were on the boat with us. When would they have time? They were in the ballroom until the scavenger hunt began. I never saw them leave."

He bit his bottom lip. "You're right. Did you see anyone leave the ballroom while we were eating?"

I opened my mouth to reply. But I stopped when I heard the shrill cry from out in the hall. At first, I thought it was the whistle of the bats. But then I realized it was a human cry. A frightened scream.

And it was joined by other screams, high cries of horror.

Brendan gripped the mannequin, as if holding himself up with it. "What *is* that?" he murmured. "What is going on?"

And then the two of us tore out of the room and went running down the long hall, toward the sound of the screams.

16.

ANOTHER NOTE

As we ran, I glanced back through the darkness to see if the bats were following us. It was too dark. I couldn't see them.

Brendan turned the corner ahead of me. I followed him, into another long hall. The screams grew louder. And as we ran closer, I saw some kids huddled in a doorway. They all stared into the pale light of a room near the end of the hall.

"What's wrong? What's happened?" Brendan shouted breathlessly.

He didn't wait for an answer. He pushed through the crowd outside the door, and I followed him. We burst into a blue-wallpapered bedroom, two twin beds against one wall.

I stumbled. And gasped when I saw the girl in the middle of the floor.

It took me a few seconds to recognize her. Patti Berger.
Oh, no. Oh, no. Please—no.

Patti on the floor. Bent in half. Eyes shut tight. Her arms and legs all twisted like a rag doll.

I took a deep breath. I felt sick. My stomach lurched. I struggled not to puke.

Brendan was muttering under his breath, his face red. His hand shook as he lifted a piece of paper. Another note. He read it out loud in a trembling voice:

"Twister, Anyone?"

I uttered a sharp cry. My whole body shuddered and I staggered back, stumbling into the other horrified kids.

"No," Brendan murmured. "This can't be happening."

He dropped down beside Patti. He spread his hand over her face. He touched her neck. He held his fingers under her nose to see if she was breathing. "No. Oh, no."

I gaped in open-mouthed silence along with the other kids. We stood together in a close pack.

Brendan lowered his head to Patti's chest and listened. With a cry, he grabbed her by the shoulders. He shook her. Shook her hard. Then he lowered her carefully to the floor. He tried to breathe into her mouth. One breath . . . two . . . three . . .

Finally, he turned away from Patti and raised his eyes to us. "This isn't a joke," he said in a hoarse whisper. "She's dead."

PART
THREE

17.

IS THERE A KILLER
IN THE HOUSE?

Kerry Reacher came bursting into the room. His long legs appeared to collapse when he saw Patti on the floor, and he dropped heavily beside her.

"What's happening? What *is* this?" Kerry's eyes were on Brendan. He didn't wait for an answer. He untwisted Patti's arms. Then he lifted her gently and pressed her face against his chest.

"No—" Brendan cried. "Don't touch her. We have to leave her for the police."

Kerry ignored him. I don't think he even heard Brendan. "She isn't dead!" Kerry screamed, holding Patti's body close. "She *can't* be dead."

Behind him, Geena and Delia were hugging each other. They both had tears running down their faces. Brendan's cousins hung back at the doorway, hands shoved in their pockets, not speaking, looking very pale and tense.

Kerry held on to Patti. Her head was tilted back on his arm. Her eyes remained shut. "Who did this?" Kerry shouted. "Who killed Patti?" He shook her body by the shoulders. "Patti—who did this? Who? I'll kill him! I swear I'll kill him." He was shaking her, shrieking at the top of his lungs.

Brendan motioned me over. "Can you help Kerry?" he whispered. "Maybe take him downstairs? He's totally freaking. We have to leave everything as we found it. When the police come . . ." His voice trailed off.

"I-I'll try," I stammered.

"I'll bring everyone else downstairs," Brendan whispered. "We have to figure out what to do."

"Why was she twisted like that?" Kerry demanded, his eyes locked on Brendan. "Who twisted her legs like that?"

Brendan lowered himself beside Kerry. "I'm so sorry," he said softly. "I'll do everything I can, Kerry. Everything—"

"I should know not to get mixed up with anyone named Fear. There's a killer in this house," Kerry declared. "A killer."

Brendan gently lifted Patti's body from Kerry's arms. He set her down. Then he helped Kerry to his feet. "Go with Rachel," he said. "Kerry? Can you hear me?"

Kerry's eyes stared blankly at the green wall. He didn't respond.

"Kerry, go with Rachel," Brendan repeated. "We'll meet you downstairs."

I put one arm around Kerry's waist and started to guide him to the door. I expected him to pull back, to fight me, or demand to stay in the room with Patti. To my surprise, he let me lead him past the other kids and into the hall.

I held onto him, and we walked together to the stairway at the end of the hall. Kerry muttered to himself, his eyes glassy, off in the distance as if he was somewhere else, seeing something I couldn't.

"The Fear family," he murmured, turning his face to me. "There's a curse. A curse on the whole family, even Brendan."

"Watch your step," I said. I grabbed him as he started to stumble.

"There's a curse on this house, too," Kerry said. "You know the story, Rachel. You have to know the story. How the Fear family had a hunting party here on the island. Like a hundred years ago. They had a hunting party and hunted all their servants. You know the story, right?"

"Well—"

"They made their servants run through the woods, and they hunted them. They shot them all. They killed all their servants. Just for a game. And they buried them somewhere in the woods."

He let out a soft cry. "It's true. It has to be true. And now look. Look what happened here. Patti. Poor Patti. Because of the curse on the Fear family."

"That's just a story. It can't be true," I said.

I suddenly pictured the mannequin that looked like Brendan swinging on the rope. Was that really a warning to Brendan? And now, Patti was dead.

A heavy feeling of dread weighed me down. *Brendan has been warned. Patti is dead. Does this mean we are ALL in danger?*

I led Kerry into the ballroom. The food table had been cleared. The waiters had left the room. But the bar table still had drinks.

The candles in the chandeliers had all been doused. Pale beams of light from spotlights in the ceiling filled the room with a silvery glow.

Two rows of folding chairs had been set up facing the fireplace. I sat Kerry down in a seat in the back row and brought him a glass of water. He stared at it as if he'd never seen water before.

"Patti . . ." he murmured. "Patti. Not you, Patti. Not you. I never should have brought you here." He raised his sad, wet eyes to me. "It's *my* fault, isn't it?"

"No," I answered. "Of course not. Don't think like that, Kerry." I motioned to the glass. "Have some water. Do you want something else? Want a beer?"

He didn't answer. He gazed into the glass. A single tear rolled down one cheek.

Suddenly, I felt like crying, too.

A wave of sadness rolled over me. I'd been trying so hard to calm Kerry down, I had been forcing down my own feelings of fright and regret. Now they came bursting to the surface, and my whole body trembled.

I'd known Patti since second grade. She was so tiny and cute and adorable. Our families were so close. So close . . . And now . . .

I lowered myself into the chair next to Kerry. The doors opened, and the rest of the party guests stampeded into the ballroom, followed by Brendan.

Brendan motioned everyone to the rows of chairs. His face was pale. His normally perfect hair was pointing in all directions. He kept his head down as he walked to the front.

"We have to get out of here," Eric Finn shouted.

"Did you call the police?" Spider demanded.

"Brendan, did you call 911?" April repeated.

Brendan shrugged. He pulled his phone from his pocket and waved it. "I can't. No bars. Remember? There's no service on the island. And the landlines have all been shut off for the winter."

"So we can't call anyone? We can't report the murder?" April asked.

The word *murder* sent a gasp through the crowd. It was as if *saying* it made it even more real and more horrible.

Once again, I pictured Patti's body all twisted up on the floor in that bedroom. And I remembered the hand-written note: *Twister, Anyone?*

Someone is playing games, I thought. *Deadly games.*

"We can't just sit here," Spider shouted. "There's a killer in the house."

"Could it be one of *us*?" Brendan's cousin Kenny asked.

"Don't be stupid," Eric snapped. "We're not killers."

"I'm not stupid," Kenny replied. He jumped to his feet. "Don't call me stupid."

Eric raised both hands as if in surrender. "Sorry. I didn't mean it. You're not stupid."

Kenny glared at him, then lowered himself to his chair.

Morgan turned to Eric. "Kenny has a short fuse," he said.

Eric stared back at him. "Was that supposed to be a warning?"

"No," Morgan said. "I was just saying."

"Who would kill Patti?" Kerry asked. "Who?" He buried his head in his hands.

"Someone strung up a dummy of me," Brendan told everyone. "It was hanging in one of the empty rooms. Swinging from the ceiling. Wearing my clothes. With a note that said something about wanting to play Hang-man."

"Sick," Delia muttered. She was hunched in her chair, twisting a strand of her white-blonde hair tensely.

"I thought the hanging dummy was some kind of warning," Brendan said. "But then . . ." He didn't finish his thought.

"Hangman and Twister," Delia said. "Someone is totally sick."

"Someone is definitely playing games with us," Geena said. "Only . . ." Her voice broke. "Murder isn't a game."

"We have to get on the boat—now," Eric said. "We have to get out of here, Brendan."

"Yes. Let's go."

"Is the boat ready?"

"We have to get off this island."

Brendan waved both hands to quiet everyone. "The boat is ready. But the pilot. Randy. He . . . He'll be okay, but he's out of commission. He's down. He can't do it. We don't have anyone to pilot the boat."

"You said you sent for someone?" Spider asked.

Geena said, "We're not totally stranded here—are we?"

"Can anyone here handle the yacht?" Eric said.

"I sent one of the workers in a speedboat back to town," Brendan said. "My family has another pilot we use in the summer. I told the worker to find him and bring him back."

"But that could be *hours*!" April protested.

"What if he doesn't find the pilot?"

"You mean we're trapped?"

Brendan waved both hands. "Calm down, everyone. I'm sure the new boat pilot is on his way. As soon as he gets here—"

Spider jumped to his feet. "Let's go now. We can figure out how to pilot the boat. How hard can it be? You turn on the engine and steer it to town."

Before anyone could move, the lights flickered, then went out.

I blinked. I stared into the glare of light that lingered. It faded. The darkness was so deep, I couldn't see Kerry sitting next to me.

Kids screamed.

I held my breath, thinking maybe the lights would flash back on.

Cries of panic rang out all around me.

"Brendan? I can't see you."

"Who turned off the lights?"

"Was it the killer?"

"Did someone just come in the room?"

"Can't anyone turn them back on?"

"Did someone cut the electricity? Brendan—help us!"

I jumped to my feet. I was too frightened just to sit there. My legs felt shaky. I forced myself to move, to get away from the chairs.

But someone grabbed my arm and started to pull me back. "Kerry?" I screamed. "Kerry? Is that *you*?"

Or is it the killer?

18.

IN THE DARK

Yes, it's me," Kerry said in a whisper. "Rachel, please don't leave me. Where were you going?"

"I . . . I just wanted to get away."

My eyes were starting to adjust to the darkness. I could see Kerry holding onto me, so frightened he didn't realize how hard he was gripping my arm. I saw other kids up on their feet.

Chairs squeaked and scraped. Frightened cries rang off the ballroom walls. I sat back down beside Kerry. He was so messed up about Patti, he couldn't move. His whole body was trembling.

Someone bumped me on the other side. Startled, I turned and found Eric beside me. He leaned close. "Are you as scared as I am?"

"Yes," I said. "I think we're all scared out of our minds."

"It's like living in a horror movie," Eric said, his voice

tight and hoarse. "I've seen this movie. Some crazed killer plans to kill us all."

"Stop it. Shut up," I said. "Don't make it worse."

"Worse? How can I make it worse?" Eric cried. "Our friend Patti is lying dead upstairs. We're sitting ducks here in the dark and . . . and—"

"Quiet, everyone! Quiet!" Brendan shouted. "Please— everyone stop talking."

It took a while for everyone to stop voicing their panic. A few kids returned to their chairs. Squinting into the heavy blackness, I could see some kids standing at the sides of the rows of seats.

"We don't know for sure that someone cut the lights. It may just be a generator down," Brendan said. "We get these blackouts here all the time."

"We have to get out of this house." I recognized April's voice, even though I couldn't see her. "We can't just stay here, Brendan."

Shouts of agreement. It took Brendan a while to get everyone quiet again. "We'll get some light," he said. "It'll make it easier. We have flashlights. My family keeps a cabinet full of flashlights for power failures like this."

"Let's get them. Let's go." Eric said.

"The cabinet is in the next room," Brendan said. "There should be a flashlight for everyone. I'll lead the way. Keep close. Keep together. It isn't far. It's a supply closet only three doors down the hall."

Chairs scraped again. Kerry stood up and led the way out of our row. He stopped to let someone move past, and Eric bumped me hard from behind.

"Oh. Sorry, Rachel."

Normally, I'd think he was doing his usual clowning. But not now.

We moved in groups of two or three toward the ballroom doorway. We had to walk slowly. The room had no windows, so the darkness was complete.

I kept close to Kerry and Eric. The hallway was just as dark as the ballroom. We turned to the left and shuffled along the carpet, following Brendan. It was like walking blindfolded.

A hush had fallen over everyone. There was nothing more to say. We were all in the same horrible situation. We were all having the same thoughts. We all had the same frantic desire to get away from this house and this island.

To escape to safety.

As we slowly moved through the hall, I thought about Patti again. She had such big plans. She was already accepted at Northwestern. She was going to be an Education major. She wanted to learn how to teach deaf children because her sister Ashlee is deaf.

Patti would have been a good teacher. She was kind and patient and very tuned in to people. And, she and Kerry planned to stay together, even though he would be at Penn, where he got a basketball scholarship.

A sob escaped my throat. I couldn't help it. I felt so much sadness, so much fear, I felt I might either explode or collapse.

Walking beside me, Eric must have sensed it. "It's okay, Rachel," he said in a low voice. "We're getting out of here. For sure."

Suddenly, I bumped into the kids in front of me. Everyone came to a sharp stop.

"I'm at the supply cabinet, everyone," Brendan announced. "I know most of you can't see me. But I have my hand on the cabinet door. And I'm opening it now. So . . . hang on . . ."

Silence. Followed by an even heavier silence.

"Whoa! What's up with this?" Brendan's startled cry. "Someone took them all. The flashlights are gone!"

19.

"THE KILLER IS PLAYING WITH US"

I held my breath. The fluttery feeling in my chest wouldn't fade.

This time, there were no cries of panic, no shouts or gasps or screams.

The only sound was the *thud* of Brendan slamming the cabinet door shut. And his murmured words: "I don't believe this."

We all knew the truth now. Someone had killed Patti. Someone had us trapped. No lights. No phones. No Internet. No one to take us home.

We were all trapped on this island and trapped inside our own thoughts, our own fears.

In horror movies, victims always scream and shriek their heads off. But I was quickly learning that panic is a private thing. You don't want to share it. You don't want others to know how terrified you are.

All your energy goes to keeping it together. Keeping yourself moving. Keeping yourself alert. But how do you decide what to do next? How can you possibly think straight when all your energy is being used to hold yourself in, to keep yourself from flying apart in a million pieces?

Delia's voice broke the tense silence. "We have to get outside. Brendan, show us the way. The sun hasn't gone down yet. When we're outside, we'll be able to see."

"But what if the killer is waiting for us outside?" Kenny Fear asked.

"Yes. This whole thing could be a trap," Spider said. "He turns off the lights and waits for us to come running out of the house."

"We can't just stay in here," I said. My voice came out tight and shrill. "We can't just stand around in the dark, waiting to see which of us is the next victim."

"We can try one of the back doors," Brendan said. "The back of the house leads into the woods. We'll be safer in the woods."

"But *then* what?" Eric demanded. "We just hide in the woods—till *when*?"

"It was getting ready to storm outside," Spider said. "We'll be soaked."

"Soaked is better than dead," Brendan said. "We can hide till the other boat pilot comes from town."

"What if he doesn't come?"

"How will he find us if we're hiding in the woods?"

"Brendan, are you sure Randy can't take us back?" Eric asked.

"Trust me," Brendan said after a pause. "Randy can't help us."

"Is he dead? Tell us the truth," Eric insisted.

Brendan didn't answer.

This started everyone talking at once. Voices were tense and hushed. I realized I was gasping for breath. The darkness suddenly felt heavy, as if someone had tossed a black wool blanket over me.

"Hey—!"

I was stunned as the hall lights flashed on. I blinked in the sudden brightness and rubbed my eyes, eager for them to adjust. Eric and I slapped a high five. Some kids cheered. Everyone started talking at once. What a relief to be able to see again.

"Maybe it *was* just a generator failure," Brendan's cousin Morgan said.

Brendan opened the empty flashlight cabinet again . . . as if he would have better luck finding the flashlights this time. "No," he said, shaking his head. "No. It wasn't a power failure. The killer is playing with us. I know it."

His words sent a chill down my back that tightened all my muscles. I wanted to run. Take off and run and not stop till I was somewhere safe.

But we all stood there, blinking in the light, as if

paralyzed, eyes on Brendan, waiting for some kind of cue, some kind of decision.

Brendan sucked in a mouthful of air. "I just remembered something," he said, eyes far away, talking more to himself than to us.

"What? What did you remember?" April darted up to him. She shook his arm hard. "Can you get us out of here? *Tell* us!"

She is nearly hysterical, I realized. *She is going to totally lose it.*

"The security room," Brendan said. He gently removed April's hand from his arm. "We have security cameras. Front and back. I know they were turned on this morning before you all arrived."

"Are there security guards, too?" Spider asked.

Brendan shook his head. "No. But the cameras may show us what's going on here. Follow me."

20.

PARTY CRASHERS

We followed him down the long hall. The faces of the Fear ancestors on the wall portraits appeared to watch us as we passed. I walked between Kerry and Eric. We didn't talk.

It was strange seeing Eric so serious, not clowning. Beads of sweat had formed across his forehead. He kept mopping the sweat off with one hand, but then more would appear.

As we turned into another hall, he frowned at me. "Are we having fun yet?"

I shuddered. "People warned me not to come here. Maybe . . . I should have listened?"

Mac's angry face flashed into my mind. He was so determined to keep me from coming to the party. I could see his jaw clenched tight, and once again, I heard his frantic pleas. *"Just don't go, Rachel. I . . . I've heard things I shouldn't."*

What did that mean?

I hadn't even thought about it till now. Mac was jealous. He couldn't stand the idea of me being with Brendan Fear. But what did he mean exactly? What had he heard?

At the end of the hall, gray light poured in through the square window onto a dark-wood door. One of the back doors. Through the glass, I could see trees blowing in a strong wind. Dead brown leaves bounced off the window.

Brendan opened the last door in the hall. It revealed a narrow room with a row of four TV monitors along a control panel with rows of dials and buttons and blinking lights.

The room wasn't big enough for us all to follow Brendan inside. We huddled in the doorway and watched as he sat down on a tall bench at the control panel.

I raised my eyes to the four screens. The pictures were in black-and-white. I figured out that two cameras were posted at the front of the house and two at the back.

"I'm going to rewind," Brendan said, "and see if we can see anything going on."

He leaned over the panel and turned some dials. I heard a low whine, and then the pictures on the four screens immediately began to scan backward.

I saw leaves blowing across the front walk. Birds landed and took off in the tall grass in the back. A squirrel raised its head as if staring into the camera. As the storm clouds hovered, the pictures darkened, then grew bright, then darkened again.

"Oh, wow," Brendan murmured. He stopped the video from rewinding. Leaning closer to the screen in front of him, he started it moving again. "Oh, wow. Oh, wow."

I grabbed Eric's shoulder as I saw the two men on the screen. Two men striding up to the backdoor. They had black ski masks over their heads. And they each had a rifle on one arm.

Hunting rifles.

I screamed as one of them raised his rifle and swung the handle at the backdoor. I could see the window glass shatter. And I watched one of the masked intruders reach in through the broken window and push open the door.

As they strode into the house, they disappeared from view.

There was no sound. We didn't need sound. We now knew exactly what was happening. Two masked men carrying hunting rifles had forced their way into Brendan's house.

They had killed Patti. But . . . why? Why were they here? What did they want? Were they on a hunting party to kill us all?

A million questions flew through my mind. Questions none of us could answer.

The masked men were here. They were somewhere in the house. And all we could do was try to get away from them.

Again, I thought of the horror movies Beth and I used

to watch. The blood would splatter and we'd laugh our heads off. Why did we think they were so much fun?

I guess because when you watch a movie, you know there isn't a chance you're actually going to die.

Brendan backed the security tape up and played it again. He squinted hard at the screen, studying the two men as they strode up to the house. He froze the picture just before one of them swung his rifle at the door.

"Who are they?" he murmured. "Who . . . ?"

He left the picture frozen on the screen and turned to us in the doorway. "Wish I knew what to do next," he said. His voice shook. He clasped his hands together to stop them from trembling. "I guess . . . I guess the main thing is not to panic."

"Not to panic?" Kenny cried. "Did you see those rifles?"

"We *have* to panic," Spider said. "We have to panic and get *out* of here!" He turned and started to the backdoor.

"We can run the boat," Kerry said. "How hard can it be? Let's go. We'll figure it out. It's our only chance."

Other kids shouted agreement. I knew Kerry was right. The boat was sitting there at the dock, waiting to take us back to town. Some of us could figure out how to pilot it. It couldn't be as dangerous as staying in this house with two masked killers.

The others raced to the door at the end of the hall. I saw Brendan pull back. He didn't climb off the stool at the control panel.

"What are you waiting for?" I cried.

He squinted at me. "Just thinking," he said. "There's a radio on the boat. We can call for help. Why didn't I think of that before?"

"Let's go," I said. I grabbed his hand and tugged him from the room. His hand was ice cold, and he staggered unsteadily as we ran.

Brendan was as terrified as the rest of us. But I knew that once we were aboard the boat and could radio for help, we'd all feel a lot better.

We burst outside, following the others into the back-yard. Tall grass stretched the width of the house. Beyond the grass, I saw the bare trees of a thick, tangled woods.

The sky was dark. Charcoal-colored clouds floated low overhead. The wind blew hard at us, as if trying to force us back.

"This way," Brendan said, motioning with one hand. The fresh air seemed to revive him, and he began to trot through the tall grass along the back of the house.

I struggled to keep up with him. Our shoes crackled the dead autumn leaves on the ground. We followed him into the deep shadow at the side of the house, making our way to the front. Before we reached the front, he motioned with both hands for us all to stop.

We stopped, breathing hard. And listened.

Were the gunmen waiting for us around the corner of the house? I could hear only the creak of tree limbs from the woods and the gusting wind whistling through the woods.

Brendan peered around the side, then motioned for us to move again. All clear.

We took off, following him down the path downhill through the trees. The dock stood at the end of the path. And the catamaran would be waiting for us at the dock.

My shoes kicked up sand as I ran full speed along the path. I knew I wouldn't feel safe until I was on that boat and speeding away from Fear Island.

Eric stumbled over an upraised tree root. His arms flailed as he caught his balance, cursing under his breath. His round face was bright red and glistening with sweat.

I ran up beside him. "Almost there," I choked out. "Almost to the dock."

He grunted in reply, his shoes thudding on the soft path.

"We're going to make it," I said. "I know we are."

And then the trees gave way to a broad open space. The path ended. The dark lake water came into view.

And I let out a horrified cry as I turned to the dock. "The boat—!"

The white catamaran bounced in the low waves as it roared away from the dock.

"Noooooo!" Eric let out an animal howl. Kids groaned and cried out. Brendan sank to his knees with a long sigh.

I ran up to the shore. I watched the boat send up a tall

white-water wake behind it as it picked up speed. Squinting hard, I could see the black-uniformed workers. About a dozen of them. They sat in the benches along the rails. Some of them stood and peered straight ahead. They never looked back.

Kerry came running to the water, shouting and waving his arms in front of him. "Stop! Come back! Come back! Stop! Can you hear me? Come back!"

We all screamed and waved and jumped up and down. But the workers weren't coming back for us. We watched them in horror. Taking the only boat. Taking our last hope of surviving.

21.

A FRIEND GOES MISSING

W hy did they leave?" Geena demanded. She had been silent the whole time. Now she glared at Brendan, more angry than frightened.

Brendan was still staring out at the dark lake, breathing hard, his hair blowing in the stiff wind.

"Why did the staff leave?" Geena asked again. "Tell us, Brendan."

He shook his head. I could see the confusion on his face.

Geena darted forward and grabbed Brendan by the shoulders. She leaned over him, her coppery hair falling over face. "Tell us the truth. Did they know the killers were coming? Is that why they got out of here?"

Brendan shook his head again. "No. I mean, how would I know? I don't know, Geena. I don't know anything. I . . . I don't understand what's happening here."

"Why didn't they come back for us?" Spider asked, his

voice shrill with fright. "If they knew what was going down, why didn't they take us, too? Why didn't they try to help us?"

"You're not telling us the truth," Geena said, holding onto Brendan's shoulders as if she wanted to shake the words out of him. "You *have* to know why the staff took off."

"N-no, I don't," Brendan stammered, finally finding his voice. "I . . . really don't." His eyes were still on the water. The boat had disappeared in the mist off the lake.

Brendan removed Geena's hands from his shoulders and climbed to his feet. "I wish I had the answer," he told her. "I wish . . ."

"What do we do now?" Delia asked. "Is there another boat we can take?"

"No. That was it," Brendan said. "The island is deserted. No one comes here in October. Especially when it's threatening rain."

I gazed up at the darkening sky. The storm clouds were black now and sliding together to block out the light. I heard a rumble of distant thunder.

"So what do we do?" Delia repeated. "There has to be a way to contact the police or someone." She shuddered. Geena moved close and put an arm around her shoulders to comfort her.

Brendan shrugged. He scratched his head. "I . . . can't think straight. I'm too weirded out. I just don't understand what these two men are doing here. How did they get here? I don't see a boat. How did they get here without a boat?"

Eric stepped up beside Brendan. "Is anyone here a good swimmer?" he asked.

Brendan squinted at him. "You mean good enough to swim across Fear Lake? That would take an hour. Maybe two with the water kicking up the way it is. And the water is freezing cold."

Eric's broad shoulders slumped. "Just a thought."

"Keep thinking," I said. "Maybe one of us will—"

I stopped when I heard a crash behind us. A heavy *thud,* coming from the house. "What was that?" I cried.

We all turned toward the house. "Was it thunder?" Brendan's cousin Morgan asked.

"Sounded more like a crash," I said. "Like something heavy falling."

"A tree maybe," Brendan said. "From the wind. Maybe a tree falling against the house?"

"This isn't getting us anywhere," Eric said, mopping sweat off his forehead. "Where are we safer? Out here or in the house?"

"Out here," a few kids said.

I felt a cold raindrop on my forehead. Then another big drop splatted the top of my head.

The rain made a pattering sound on the ground as it

started to come down harder. The cold wind swirled, splashing water on us on all sides.

We had run out of the house without raincoats or umbrellas. I hugged myself, shivering. "Maybe we can think better in the house," I said.

There wasn't any debate. We all took off, heads down, leaning into the wind, following the path up through the trees to the house. A jagged bolt of lightning crackled to our left, lighting up the trees, followed by a deafening explosion of thunder.

Breathing hard, I leaned forward and kept running. The house came into view at the top of the slope. It rose up in front of us, dark and ominous against an even darker sky.

Struggling to keep my balance, I slipped on the long, slick grass. My shoes sank into the soft mud underneath. Brendan led the way, swinging his arms as he ran, and I followed close behind him.

What was that loud crash we heard? I didn't see any sign of a tree crashing onto the house.

Brendan reached the front door first. Grabbed the brass door handle and tugged the door open.

I held back. Were the masked killers waiting for us there?

The front entryway was empty. I followed Brendan into the house, shaking off rainwater, hugging myself to stop the shivers. My hair was soaked and was slipping out of my ponytail. I swept it back and tried to force it back into the elastic band. We were all totally drenched and bedraggled, our faces tight with fear.

Eric had his arm around April. She had her head down, her shoulders shaking. Geena and Spider huddled close in silence. No one spoke. I knew we were all listening. Concentrating. Alert for any sign of the two intruders.

"This way," Brendan said, motioning us down the hall. He led the way back to the ballroom. Our footsteps echoed in the big, empty room. Harsh yellow light poured down from spotlights in the ceiling. The food and drink tables were empty. The fire had died in the big fireplace.

Brendan called his two cousins to the fireplace, pointed to the wood stacked at the side, and asked them to rebuild the fire. "I'll check out the kitchen. Maybe I can make some hot chocolate for everyone." He disappeared through a door to our right.

A warm drink was a good idea. I couldn't stop shivering. I dropped into a folding chair beside Eric and April and hugged myself, trying to get warm. My beautiful jacket was soaked. I took it off and draped it over the arm of an empty chair.

"I'll bet there are a lot of ghosts in this ballroom," Eric said. "Ghosts of the evil Fear family. Do you think they are watching us?"

"Eric, shut up," I snapped. "Do you really think this is the right time for ghost stories?"

"We all know the story of the Fears," Eric continued, ignoring me. "We all know the family is cursed. And now we're part of their story. Maybe we're cursed, too."

He turned to Brendan's cousins. "You two are Fears. Do you know something you're not telling us?"

Kenny and Morgan scowled at him. "Do we look like killers to you?" Morgan said.

"Yeah. You do," Eric replied.

"Shut up, Eric!" several kids shouted.

"Eric, you're so stupid," Geena said. "What are you trying to do? Do you really think accusing them will help us? You're not helping anyone."

"Why don't *you* go swim the lake and get help?" Spider suggested.

"Why don't you make me?" Eric shot back.

"Stop being a total baby," Geena said. "We have to be serious."

"Your *face* is serious," Eric said.

I knew what Eric was doing. It was his only way of dealing with tension. Make jokes. Try to be funny.

"Eric, sure hope you're not the next victim," Spider said. "We'd miss you. Seriously."

That made some kids gasp. I knew Spider didn't have much of a sense of humor. He didn't like Eric's jokes. But

Spider was being extra-nasty now. Probably because he was so frightened.

Eric jumped to his feet and faced Spider. "Won't you feel terrible if I *am* the next victim?"

"I'll cry like a baby," Spider said sarcastically.

Eric charged at him. The two boys pulled each other to the floor and started to wrestle. I screamed. "Stop it! STOP it! This is *crazy!*"

Brendan's cousin Kenny ran from the fireplace, grabbed Spider by the shoulders, and pulled him off Eric. Eric rolled away, his face bright red, a trickle of blood on his lips.

Brendan returned carrying a tray of cups. He set them on the table. His mouth opened in surprise. "What's up? What's happening?"

"Spider and I were just goofing," Eric said, wiping the blood off his mouth with a shirtsleeve. "You know. Messing around."

Kenny let go of Spider. Spider glared at Eric but didn't say anything. Finally, he turned away and strode quickly to the table. He grabbed a cup of hot chocolate and walked to the other side of the room.

"Have some hot chocolate, everyone," Brendan said, his eyes still on Eric. "I think I made enough for everyone And I found some sweatshirts and sweaters, help yourself."

I walked over to the table and took the smallest sweatshirt I could find. I slipped it on and then took one of the steaming cups. I held the cup in both hands, letting it warm them.

Eric's lip was still bleeding. Spider stood against the wall, massaging his shoulder. He must have hurt it in their scuffle.

The hot chocolate disappeared quickly. Without anyone saying anything, we all took seats on the folding chairs, as if getting ready for a meeting. Brendan paced back and forth in front of us.

His cousins were fiddling with the fire. I was surprised they didn't try harder to get acquainted with any of us from Shadyside High. They pretty much kept to themselves. Of course, we were all too frightened to be social now.

"I don't really know what to say," Brendan started. He had his hands jammed deep in his pockets. "Maybe if we all think hard . . ."

I was near the back of the seats. I glanced around at the other kids in front of me. My eyes went back and forth. I stopped briefly at each one.

Then, I felt my heart skip a beat. I let my eyes wander over the kids again. And then one more time, my panic rising, tightening my throat till I could barely breathe.

I jumped to my feet. "Hey," I shouted. "Where's Kerry?"

Brendan stopped pacing. Kids turned to look at me.

"Where's Kerry Reacher?" I cried. "Has anyone seen Kerry?"

22.

ANOTHER GAME

Kerry?" I shouted, my voice cracking. "Kerry? Are you here?"

Silence.

"I didn't see him outside," Brendan said. "Did anyone see him when we ran to the dock?"

"Yes, he was outside with us," I said. "I ran right beside him. I know he was there when we saw the boat leaving with the staff. But then when it started to rain . . ." My voice trailed off.

I thought hard. "I . . . didn't see him run back to the house," I said.

Brendan scratched his head. "He stayed outside in the rain? No way. He wouldn't. Would he?"

No one answered. I shut my eyes and tried to picture running back through the rain to the house. Was Kerry still beside me? No. No, he wasn't.

"I knew he was totally messed up about Patti," Brendan said. "But he seemed to be getting it together. Why would he stay outside by himself? He had to come back into the house. I know he's here somewhere."

"Stop talking!" I cried. "Talking isn't going to find him. We have to look for him!"

"Rachel is right," Brendan said. "Should we split up?" He paused. "No. Better not. We'll go together. We can't search outside. It's a downpour. We'll start on the first floor of the house. And then go up a floor at a time."

A frightened hush fell over everyone as we started to the ballroom door. I hurried to catch up to Brendan.

"We'll find him," Brendan said softly. "Maybe he just got lost. This house is so confusing, and he wasn't thinking clearly. I'm sure he's okay."

But I could hear the fear in his voice. He kept his head down and didn't look me in the eye.

As we followed the long hall, I kept picturing Kerry on the boat when we sailed to Fear Island, his arm around Patti. I kept picturing how happy they both looked. How funny they looked together—a tiny doll with a giant basketball player.

We walked through the brightly lit kitchen. The workers had left it a mess, with dirty pans and stacks of unwashed pizza trays, dirty glasses piled in the sink. The countertops were grease-stained and cluttered with scraps of uneaten food.

No sign of Kerry.

Behind the kitchen were several rooms for maids and kitchen workers. We searched them all. Then we turned a hall that led toward the back of the house.

"Hey, stop shoving!" Spider shouted from behind me.

"I didn't shove you. I didn't touch you," I heard Eric reply.

Brendan spun around. "Let's stick together, guys." He raised his hand for us to come to a stop. "Kerry won't be back here. It's all construction. My parents are building a big shed and boat hangar back here. I think we should turn around and—"

"No," I interrupted. "Let's check it out. We have to look everywhere."

Brendan hesitated. I gave him a gentle push toward the backdoor. "Okay. You're right," he said. He pushed open the door, and we followed him out to the construction site.

The rainstorm had been short. The rain had stopped but the heavy clouds lingered, hanging low over the trees. I squinted into the eerie gray-green light.

The ground was covered with long concrete slabs to build the hangar foundation, I guessed. They were stacked neatly in rows across the dirt, about six or eight feet high.

One pile looked as if it had fallen. The long slabs were tilted over each other at weird angles.

Was that the crash we heard? I wondered. *The sound of these slabs toppling over?*

My eyes moved down to the bottom of the pile. I blinked. I felt a sharp jolt of shock run down my body. I tried to scream but no sound came out.

I stared at the legs poking out from under the fallen slabs.

The long legs.

Kerry's legs.

Oh, no. Oh, please no.

The rest of him . . . crushed . . .

A concrete slab lay over the middle of his body. His stomach . . . his chest . . . crushed beneath its weight. His legs sprawled from one side of the boulder. I could see his neck and head on the other.

I couldn't move. I couldn't breathe. *This isn't happening.*

Brendan dove toward Kerry. He picked up a sheet of paper from the top of a concrete slab. He read it out loud: *"I Never Was Good at Jenga."*

Brendan crushed the paper in his fist and tossed it to the ground. Then he lowered himself to his knees. Bent over Kerry. He grabbed Kerry's head in both hands. He tried to hold it up. But then he set it gently back onto the ground.

Brendan climbed to his feet and turned to us, his face pale, his chin quivering. "Kerry is dead," he said. "He's dead, too."

23.

A GHOSTLY INVITATION

O ur horrified cries rang out over the construction site. They echoed through the trees at the back of the yard.

April and Geena held onto each other. They both were sobbing, tears running down their flushed faces. Muttering to himself, Spider angrily kicked a clump of dirt across the ground. Delia shut her eyes and hugged herself.

I grabbed Eric's arm and held on. I had the feeling my legs were going to collapse. I pulled Eric to the side. We both turned away from the sight of Kerry's sneakers on the ground, his legs jutting out from beneath the heavy slab.

"First they kill someone. Then they leave a stupid note. It's so sick," Brendan said.

"We know who is writing them," I said. "We saw them break into the house. But—*why*? Why are they killing us? What do they want?" My voice cracked again.

Eric moved away from me. I watched him walk off to be by himself at the side of the house. I could feel my panic rising, like the ocean tide climbing higher . . . higher. I suddenly felt like I couldn't breathe, like I was about to drown.

I felt a hand on my shoulder. I turned to see Brendan, studying me, his face filled with concern. "You okay?"

"No," I said. "Not really." A tear rolled down my cheek.

He held onto me. "What are we going to do?"

I couldn't answer. I just stared at him. He looked totally lost. His eyes kept darting around crazily.

"I should ask if *you're* okay," I said. "You don't look so good."

I let out a short cry of surprise as he wrapped his arms around me and hugged me. His cheek felt blazing hot against mine. He let go quickly and turned away as if embarrassed. He didn't say a word. I watched him walk over to Eric, taking long strides.

I rubbed my face. I could still feel the heat of his cheek on mine.

Weird.

That was not what I expected.

Eric turned to Brendan, his expression tense. His hands were balled into tight fists. "What are we going to do?" he demanded. "What is the plan here?"

Brendan lowered his head. "I don't have a plan. I . . .

I'm trying to think of a way to get us home safely. But . . ." His voice trailed off.

"Should we search the island?" Eric asked. "See if anyone else came here this weekend? Someone who could help us?"

"The island is empty," Brendan said. "I know this for a fact. There are only eight other houses on the island. And a few fishing cottages. No one here."

"But maybe someone left a boat we can use," Spider said.

"The boats have all been taken up for winter," Brendan answered. "And no one else has a catamaran or a boat big enough for all of us."

"But even if there's a canoe . . ." Spider insisted, rubbing a hand tensely through his curly brown hair. "Someone could take it to town and get help."

Brendan shook his head. "No one leaves canoes out after the season."

Kenny took a few steps toward Brendan. "We could break into a garage or a shed. Take a canoe."

"That's not as easy as it sounds," Brendan told him. "We'd need tools to break locks."

Kenny scowled at his cousin. "We have to try *something*. Do you want to get out of here or not?"

"I want to get away from here as much as you do," Brendan said. "Think I want to stay here and watch us get picked off one by one? I'm thinking hard, Kenny. I'm thinking as hard as I can."

Kenny took a few steps toward Brendan, as if challenging him. "And what are you thinking, Brendan?"

Brendan hesitated. "I'm thinking we need to stick together. We need to stick close together. Keep an eye on everyone."

Kenny laughed . . . a harsh, scornful laugh. "Stick together? That's the best you can do?"

"Take it easy, Kenny," Morgan said. "Picking a fight with Brendan isn't going to help anyone."

"Brendan always was a wimp," Kenny muttered. "Stick together. That's the best Fearless Leader can do. Two people are dead. Someone is playing a game with us. Writing those notes. Someone thinks that killing us is . . . is . . . funny."

Brendan sighed. "Patti and Kerry . . . They went off on their own," he said. "I'm only saying it's safer to stay with the group."

"Maybe we could hide in one of the other houses or cabins on the island," April suggested. "It wouldn't be so hard to break into a house, right? We could hide till the new boat pilot arrives."

"But what if there *is* no new boat pilot?" Kenny demanded.

The discussion continued, but I couldn't bear to hear

any more. I covered my ears with my hands. I had a loud buzzing in my head. Tension. Tension and panic.

I couldn't stand there one more second. I couldn't stand there seeing Kerry's legs stretching out from under the slab. Kerry's crushed body underneath.

I started to back away from the others. My head spinning, I reached the house and went inside. I pushed the door closed behind me. The buzzing in my ears faded. So did the voices of my friends.

Are any of us going to survive?

Are any of us going to get off this island and back to our homes?

I tried to force the questions from my mind. But how could I?

I gazed down the long hall, dark as a tunnel. I couldn't hear a sound over the low buzzing in my ears. My throat ached again. I felt like I was choking. I had to get water.

I started down the hall, trying to remember how to get back to the ballroom. My legs felt unsteady as I walked. My knees wouldn't work. I had to force myself forward.

I knew Brendan said we should stick together. But my throat was throbbing. I really needed water.

My footsteps scraped softly in the empty hall. I kept glancing from side to side, expecting someone to jump out at me. My parched throat throbbed.

I turned a corner, peered into the inky darkness—and stopped.

A thin rectangle of light escaped the room in front of me. The door was nearly closed. I froze and listened hard. My whole body tingled with fear.

Someone was in that room.

I forced myself to the edge of the doorway. Stepping into the beam of light, I pushed the door open a few inches more. Peering inside, I could see tall shelves of books against the wall. This was some kind of library or study.

I gripped the side of the door. I wanted to slide it open more so that I could see the front of the room. But in my fear, I slipped—and pushed the door all the way open.

I stumbled into the room—and stared at the woman behind a long table. I had to squint. She stood in a gray mist, as if the room was filled with fog.

She didn't look up at the sound of my clumsy entrance. I gazed at her scraggly white hair down to her shoulders. She had tiny black eyes over a long, pointed nose. She wore a gray, high-necked blouse over a long gray skirt. Her face, her skin all matched, the same gray as her clothing.

She had no color at all. As if I was staring at a black-and-white photo. She kept billowing in and out of focus as I studied her through the mist.

She stood behind the table, head down, working on something. I focused on the table—and held my hand over my mouth to keep from uttering a cry.

The table was covered with animal parts. I saw squirrel

heads and a pile of squirrel tails. A cat's head. A stack of gleaming, round eyeballs. Claws. Paws. And a small, black dog's body without legs.

I couldn't breathe. I couldn't stop myself. I took a step forward on trembling legs. And then another, watching her lowered head, her hand slowly moving back and forth.

As I drew closer, the fog seemed to lift. And I saw what she was working on so intently.

One side of her blouse was raised. And I could see a long, narrow opening in her skin under her ribs. She had a black needle in her hand—and she was stitching the opening in her body, sewing the skin together.

Victoria Fear?

The ghost of Victoria Fear?

I didn't want to believe it. But there she was. I was watching her sew herself together.

I wanted to scream. I wanted to run. But before I could make a move, she raised her gray face, the patchy white hair falling against her drawn cheeks.

She saw me. Her mouth tilted into a jagged smile. She raised the long needle, the black thread trailing beneath it.

"Come closer, dear." Her voice was as dry as wind rattling dead, brown leaves. "Come closer. It won't hurt for long. I promise."

24.

ANOTHER INTRUDER

I finally found my voice. A scream burst from my throat. I spun away from her, that long needle and the slender rip in her side lingering in my mind.

I took off running, out the door, into the hall. My head spinning, the floor tilted up to meet me. *Which way? Which way?*

I finally remembered. I turned the corner and, breathing hard, ran full speed toward the back door. I didn't slow up when I saw the other kids trudge into the house, led by Brendan.

Brendan stopped short when he saw me barreling toward him. His mouth dropped open. "Rachel? Where were you? What's wrong?"

"Victoria Fear!" I cried breathlessly, gasping for breath, straining to get the words out.

Brendan hugged me. "Whoa. I'm glad you're okay."

The others stared in confusion.

I took a step back, my heart racing. "Victoria Fear! I saw her!" I cried. "A ghost. A ghost, Brendan. I saw Victoria Fear's ghost."

Brendan shook his head. "Rachel, I'm not getting this. You saw the security video. We have two murderers in the house. Why are you doing this ghost thing?"

"I . . . I saw her," I insisted.

The others chimed in, everyone talking at once. "Rachel, did you hit your head?"

"You saw a ghost? Have you totally lost it?"

"Is she okay? Is she in shock because of Kerry?"

Brendan stepped forward and tried to pull me into another hug. But I pushed his arms away. The words burst out of me in a torrent. "You've got to believe me. I saw her. I saw the animals she was stuffing. And she was sewing . . . sewing herself up. Brendan, she—"

He pressed a finger over my mouth. "Show us," he said. "Rachel, take a deep breath. Then show us. Take us there."

I followed his instruction. I took a deep breath, held it in, then let it go. But it didn't calm me. "She was a ghost, Brendan. I saw her. I'm not crazy."

The other kids stared at me, murmuring to themselves. April stepped up to me. "You're in shock, Rachel. We all are. But we can't start seeing ghosts. We need to—"

"Show us," Brendan repeated. "Show us the room. Where did you see the ghost?"

"It . . . it had all these bookshelves," I stammered. "And she stood behind a long table."

"The library on the first floor?" Brendan said. "Okay. Follow me."

He took long strides down the hall. I hurried to keep up with him. The others followed, silent now.

We turned the corner. I saw the room, the door still open, the bright rectangle of light tilting out onto the hall floor.

"That's it," I whispered. "She's in there."

We stopped a few feet from the door, as if bracing ourselves for what we were about to see. Then Brendan and I stepped into the room together. We gazed at the tall bookshelves. Then we both turned to the front of the room.

I let out a sharp cry.

"There's no one in here," Brendan said.

The other kids had crept into the room and stood huddled against the bookshelves on the back wall.

"No," I whispered. "I saw her."

"No one here," Brendan said, still staring at the front of the room. At the long table, which was bare. Completely bare. The dark wood gleaming under the ceiling light.

Brendan turned to me. I couldn't read his expression. Was he worried about me?

"I didn't imagine it," I said. "She was in here. She had animal parts . . . A dog's body. She stood right there."

I turned and saw the other kids studying me intently. No one said a word. But I could read their thoughts.

Rachel has lost it.

Rachel is seeing ghosts.

Rachel is crazy.

"I'm not crazy!" I screamed. And then I turned and bolted toward the door. Without thinking, without even realizing what I was doing, I pushed past April and Geena, shoved them out of my way, and burst out into the hall.

I had to get away. I had to escape their eyes, their hard expressions, judging me, feeling sorry for me. Poor Rachel, who has lost her mind.

I ran blindly down the hall, turned, and kept running down another long hall. This one dark except for pale gray light filtering in from a high window at the far end.

I could hear Brendan calling my name, shouting for me to stop.

But I kept running.

Kept running until I saw something. Or someone.

A blur. Just a blur of color against the gray light. Someone crossed the hall up ahead of me. Someone running fast.

And I recognized him. Even in the darkness, I recognized him. But it was impossible. It couldn't be.

Mac? Mac Garland?

No. No way.

Why would Mac be here?

"Hey—Mac?" I shouted his name. I took off, running again. "Mac? Is that you? I saw you!"

Did he follow me here?

Why?

Maybe I was wrong. Maybe it wasn't Mac. But I thought I recognized his straight, dark-blond hair. Recognized the way he stands straight up when he runs. (I once told him he ran like a giraffe.)

"Mac? I saw you! Mac?" My voice rang off the hallway walls, shrill and high.

Peering into the darkness, I slowed to a stop. No sign of him. I'd lost him somehow. Did I make a wrong turn? Was he hiding in one of the rooms?

I bent over and put my hands on my knees. I took a deep breath, then another, trying to get my heart to stop pounding.

I straightened up, my heart still racing. I gasped when I heard rapid footsteps. Hard thuds. Behind me. Coming fast.

"Huh?" I whirled around.

And saw someone running hard, hands outstretched as if to grab me. A man in a black mask.

25.

MORE SCREAMS

I froze with a gasp. I raised my arms in front of me, shielding myself. Too late to run. Too late. I squeezed my hands into tight fists. Could I fight him off?

"Rachel?" He called to me. And as he hurtled closer, I saw that it wasn't a masked man, after all. His face had been covered by the deep shadow of the hallway.

"Brendan!" I shouted. "I . . . I'm so glad it's you."

He ran up to me, breathing hard. "Rachel, why did you run away? What are you doing here?"

"I . . . thought I saw someone," I stammered. "Someone running really fast, and I thought—"

"You shouldn't ever leave the group," Brendan said. He locked his eyes on mine. "You know you'll be safer if you stay with everyone."

"Oh, Brendan," I sighed. I threw my arms around him. "I'm so . . . frightened." I pressed my face against his cheek.

He wrapped his arms around me and pulled me to him. He held me tight and lowered his face to mine. We kissed. A long, sweet kiss. Sweet but desperate. As if we were trying to force away all the horror.

He ended the kiss and narrowed his eyes at me. He didn't say anything for a long moment. I could see there was something he wanted to say. Finally, he whispered, "You'll be safe, Rachel. You'll be safe from them."

I blinked. "How do you know?"

He didn't answer. He leaned forward and kissed me again. I shut my eyes. I really did want the rest of the world to go away.

But we both pulled back when we heard the screams. Hoarse cries of horror, echoing down the hall.

A chill shook my body. I was still holding onto Brendan. I didn't want to let go.

But another outburst of screams made us pull apart. We both turned toward the sound.

"Please . . . not again," I whispered. "Not another murder."

26.

THE NEXT VICTIM

We followed the screams to a den near the front of the house. The room was in water colors, all blues and greens. Two green leather couches faced a big widescreen TV on one wall.

In the far corner, a small round table had been knocked on its side. In its place stood a low wooden ladder. Brendan and I pushed through the screaming, crying kids to get a better look.

"Nooooooo!" I slapped my hands to the sides of my face. My stomach churned. I struggled to keep my lunch down.

"Eric! Not Eric!" I wailed.

But yes. Eric Finn was draped upside down over the ladder. His head was bright purple, down near the floor. His arms drooped limply at his sides. His shoes were jammed between the two top rungs.

"The note! There's a note!" I cried.

Brendan stood frozen in horror. I grabbed the note off the bottom ladder rung and read it:

"Chutes and Ladders Isn't Always a Baby Game."

I let out a shuddering cry. The sheet of paper fell from my hand and fluttered to the floor beside the ladder. Backing away, I thought I saw Eric's fingers twitch. "Is he still alive?" The words burst from my throat in a voice I didn't recognize. Brendan lurched forward and grabbed Eric's hand. He squeezed it. He shook his head. "Ice cold. But he hasn't been dead that long—has he?"

The room erupted in frightened voices and soft sobs.

Eric dead, too.

And who would be next?

I turned my gaze to the blue-green wallpaper. I couldn't bear to look at Eric hanging there upside down, his blond hair tumbling over his face. I couldn't believe I'd never hear his voice again. Never hear him make another joke.

Again, I was desperate to escape. I backed out of the room. I still had my hands pressed to my cheeks. My stomach churned like a washing machine in spin cycle.

Brendan was gently lifting Eric's body off the ladder. Huddled in small groups of two and three, everyone watched. No one moved to help him.

I backed to the door, my shoes scraping the soft carpet. I lowered my hands to my sides. I balled them into tight fists.

This can't be happening.

I stepped into the hall, backed away from the door, away from the horror—and someone grabbed me from behind.

Strong hands gripped my shoulders and pulled me into the hall.

I started to scream. But a hand slid roughly over my mouth. The palm pressed hard over my lips, silencing me.

I ducked and squirmed and tried to twist away. And as I fought, I realized: *It's me. I'm the next victim.*

27.

THE FINAL CURTAIN

Struggling to free myself, I ducked my head and jerked my body forward with all my strength. The hands slid off me, and I stumbled into the wall.

Gasping for breath, I spun around. And stared at Mac Garland.

"Mac! What are you doing here?" I choked out.

He was breathing hard, too. His dark-blond hair fell over his forehead. He narrowed his metal-gray eyes at me.

"Mac—you *hurt* me," I cried. "Why are you here?" And then the words poured out like a gushing waterfall. "I saw you running. I knew it was you. What's going on? Tell me!"

He glanced up and down the long hall. "I'll explain later," he said in a breathless whisper. "Hurry."

"Hurry?" I cried. "What do you mean? What do you want, Mac? Answer my questions? What are you doing here? Did you follow me?"

"Later," he repeated. He reached for me again, but I backed away. "Come with me, Rachel. I told you. I told you things were going down."

"The murders? You *knew* about them last week?"

He didn't answer. He pushed the hair off his forehead with one hand. Then he burst forward and grabbed my hand. He tugged hard. "Let's go."

"No! Let *go* of me!" I cried. "Let go! The murders, Mac. You knew about them?"

He scowled at me. He's a good-looking guy, but he's ugly when he's angry. "Shut up," he snapped, glancing up and down the hall again. "I don't know what you're talking about."

"Somebody—help me!" I tried to scream to the kids back in the den, but the words came out in a choked whisper.

"Don't be an idiot," he rasped. "Shut up and come with me. *Now.* I have a canoe, Rachel. I can get you out of here."

I spun free and took several steps back. "I . . . I'm not going anywhere with you. Answer my questions. What do you know about the murders?"

"We've got to hurry, Rachel. I'll explain later. There's no time."

His chest was heaving up and down. He took rapid, wheezing breaths. I'd seen him angry before, but I'd never seen him this desperate.

"I'm not going with you," I said. I gritted my teeth and tensed my whole body, preparing to make a run for it. Mac stood in the middle of the hall. I'd have to fake him out somehow to get past him.

Brendan and the others were still in the den down the hall. I knew I was just a few yards from safety.

"I'm warning you," Mac said, his eye twitching. His face was red, in a rage. "I'm warning you. I know what's going down. Rachel—I'll get you out of here. But you've got to go now. Come on!"

I stared at him, thinking hard, frantically trying to plan a strategy.

If I dart to the left, maybe I can get him to move left. Then I'll throw him off-balance by running to the right.

I took a deep breath, readying myself to run. And then I saw something in Mac's eyes. He wasn't watching me. His gaze went over my shoulder to something down the hall.

His expression changed. His eyes went wide with fear. And to my surprise, Mac swung away from me and took off, running in the other direction. Before I could utter a sound, he disappeared around a corner.

"Weird," I said. My heart fluttered in my chest. I turned and gazed down the dark hall. I didn't see anything. I used the wall to shove off and stumbled on shaky legs back to the den with the others.

"Brendan—" I gasped.

He spun around at my cry. "Rachel? Did you leave again?"

"I—I-I—" I stammered, picturing Mac, his eyes so wide and crazy.

Brendan didn't give me a chance to say anything. "Follow me," he said. "We need to regroup. Think about our next move."

I glimpsed Eric's body stretched out on the couch. His mouth had dropped open and his eyes were rolled up in his head.

A stab of sheer terror tightened my throat. I followed Brendan as he led everyone down the long hall, then down another. He kept his eyes straight ahead and took long, rapid strides as if desperate to get away from that room, from the sight of Eric so still and dead.

Brendan led us to a large room we hadn't seen before. A blue curtain stretched along the back wall. Armchairs and couches faced the curtain. It was obviously a theater or a screening room.

Brendan motioned to the chairs and couches. "Take a seat, everyone. We need to talk."

Kenny and Morgan dropped onto the couch near the back of the room. I slumped into a brown leather armchair at one side. Spider sat on the wide arm of my chair. "This can't be happening," he whispered. "Someone has to come and save us . . . before . . . before . . ." His voice trailed off.

I knew what he was going to say. *Before we are all killed one by one.*

Geena and April didn't sit. They stood leaning tensely against one wall, their arms tightly crossed in front of their chests. Geena had been tensely chewing her bottom lip, and now a trickle of bright red blood ran down her chin.

Brendan stepped in front of the curtain and began to pace back and forth. Finally, he stopped and turned to us. "This was always a happy room for my family," he said. "This is our little theater, where we used to put on plays when we were kids, and we had funny talent shows."

He sighed. "A lot of good times in this room. But . . . I guess I could say this is the final curtain."

He walked to the far end of the curtain. He grabbed a slender rope in both hands and began to pull it. And as he pulled, the curtains parted in the middle and slowly slid open.

Gasps of shock filled the room as we saw what was behind the curtain. And then the gasps turned to screams when we realized we were staring at three bodies.

The bodies of our friends. Patti, Kerry, and Eric. Face down. Piled in a heap on top of each other.

"How . . . how did they get here?" I cried, my voice hoarse with terror. "Who did this? Brendan—who moved them here?"

I tried to look away. But the horrifying sight held me as if in a trance.

Eric on the bottom. Kerry on top of him, his long legs bent at an odd angle. Patti sprawled face down on top of Kerry, arms hanging limply to the floor, her hair falling over her lifeless face.

"No . . . No . . ." I shook my head as if trying to shake away the sickening scene. "No . . ."

And as I stared, gripped in horror, the pile of bodies started to move.

28.

THE PARTY'S OVER

Patti moaned and slowly raised her head.

Kerry's hands twitched. His big sneakers slid against the floor.

Eric turned his face toward us and blinked.

My heart skipped a beat. I couldn't breathe. I jumped to my feet.

No one screamed or cried out. No one made a sound.

I felt the blood pulsing at my temples. I pressed my hands to the sides of my face.

"The dead RISE!" Kerry groaned. "Awake! Awake!"

Patti pushed herself off Kerry's back and stood up. She pushed her hair into place and adjusted her T-shirt.

Still on the floor, Eric grinned at us. "Did we fool you? Did you fall for it?"

Kerry stood up and stretched his long arms over his head. "How'd it go, Brendan?"

Finally, we found our voices. The room filled with

screams of shock, mixed with happiness, mixed with anger.

I could feel my brain doing flip-flops. I had to shut my eyes for a moment.

They're alive?

This was all a joke? All unreal? All this horror?

Brendan nodded to the three ex-corpses. "Good job, dudes. Game over."

"Brendan? What's up?" Spider shouted. " 'Game over'?"

Brendan turned to face us. "You've all been playing my new party game," he said. "I created it for this party. Know what I call it? Total Panic."

Brendan grinned at us. He looked very pleased with himself.

No one reacted to the news. I think we were too stunned. I felt like I was in shock.

Brendan snickered. "Guys? Are you okay? Maybe my game was *too* good."

I took a deep breath and finally found my voice. "Are you saying nothing that happened this afternoon was real?"

He nodded. "I planned everything. I wanted Total Panic to be the scariest party game ever."

My confusion was lifting. I started to feel my chest tighten with anger. "Well, you scared us to death. We all thought—" He didn't let me finish. He raised a hand to silence me.

"I planned everything," he repeated. "I even planted the dead animals in your beds to get you in a frightened mood before the party."

"It was *you*?" Geena cried.

"Well . . . Eric and Kerry helped me. All part of the game. I planned the three murders. I planned Randy hitting his head and the fake blood in the water. I planned the lights going out, the missing flashlights, the masked men breaking in on the security camera, the servants all leaving and taking the boat with them."

"All a game?" Spider cried. "Are you *kidding* me? All a game?"

"Brendan—I don't believe you!" Geena cried. "You told us Patti, Kerry, and Eric were dead. But—"

"It was all a game, Geena," Brendan said. "Seriously. I was the only one to examine the bodies—remember? I was always the one who announced they were dead. I never gave anyone a chance to get up close to them."

The room filled with angry murmurs and words of disbelief.

"As you can see, everyone is okay," Brendan said. "Well . . . except for Eric. He's always been a little weird."

"Hey, aren't you all happy to see me alive?" Eric cried.

"No way," Spider said. "We liked you better as a corpse."

That made everyone laugh, breaking the almost unbearable tension.

"It really *was* a game," I blurted out. "All a game to frighten us to death." My voice cracked. I felt so furious at Brendan for frightening me—and everyone—so badly.

"Brendan—you went too far!" Geena cried.

"It was *too* scary," his cousin Morgan agreed. "Did you want to give us all heart attacks?"

Brendan snickered. "I didn't want to put you in the hospital. I just wanted to see if I could really terrify you."

"It's not funny. It's *mean*," Geena said angrily.

"It's sick," April agreed. "Totally sick. You have a sick mind, Brendan."

"I take that as a compliment," Brendan said. "I guess my game worked."

Everyone started talking at once, shouting at Brendan.

"You made us look like idiots."

"This isn't a party. We were just guinea pigs for your sick game."

"You can't play with people's emotions like that. It's totally cruel."

"It's sick, Brendan. You're way sick."

We were all so angry, it was like we forgot to be happy that our friends were actually still alive.

As the shouts and curses and angry words continued, I watched Brendan. His eyes flashed with excitement, and he kept a broad smile on his face. He was totally enjoying our reaction to his terrifying game.

I tried to figure out the answer to the one question that

I couldn't chase away: *Is he some kind of creative genius, or is he a dangerous sicko?*

I suddenly realized that Patti, Kerry, and Eric must have been planning this whole thing with Brendan that night in the back booth at Lefty's, the night Brendan invited me to the party. That's what they were talking about so intensely that night. They were planning the murder scenes, planning the whole thing.

And then a flash of anger made me grit my teeth. Was Brendan only *pretending* to like me? Was that a game, too?

I suddenly felt like a total fool.

Maybe *everything* was a game with Brendan. When he invited me to the party . . . when he chose me as his scavenger hunt partner . . . when he held me and kissed me. . . . All a game? All a joke to him?

My fists were clenched into such tight balls, my nails dug into my palm. I took a deep breath and tried to let the hot anger wash out of me.

Eric bumped up against me, a toothy grin on his face. "Rachel, were you scared?"

"Terrified," I said. "We all were. Brendan's game was sadistic and mean."

Eric grinned. "I thought it was a hoot. When he told us his plan, I split a gut laughing. Brendan is a mad genius."

"I'm not so sure," I said. "But I . . . I'm glad to see you're alive."

Eric wrapped his beefy arms around me. "Rachel, I didn't know you cared."

"Don't get crazy," I said, pushing him away. "I'm glad you're alive, but I'm never going to speak to you again."

Brendan was waving his arms, trying to get everyone quiet. "Relax, guys. Come on. Everybody chill."

"You owe us all an apology," someone said. "I'm going to have nightmares for a year."

Brendan's two cousins glared at him angrily. "Does Uncle Oliver know about this game?" Morgan asked.

"You should have told us about it. We're family," Kenny said, shaking his head.

Brendan shrugged in reply. "Okay, I hear you. I hear you," he shouted over the angry voices. "You can all chill now. I . . . I wanted to give you an exciting night. You know. A game you'll remember."

"You guys have no sense of humor!" Eric cried. "Admit it. It was a blast."

"Murder isn't a game, Eric," Spider said.

The grumbling and angry shouts continued.

Brendan waved his arms again, trying for silence. "Come on, guys. Just let it go. Relax. The staff will be back in an hour or two with the boat. If you want to leave then, fine. No problem."

He blinked. "Oh, wait. I have one more surprise." He glanced at me. He shouted toward the door. "Are you guys there?"

We all turned to see Randy stride into the room, his white admiral's cap tilted over his head. "Surprise!" he shouted.

He was followed by a young woman. She was dressed in an old-fashioned high-necked blouse and long gray skirt. She carried a white-haired wig in her hands.

It took me a few seconds to realize I was staring at Victoria Fear.

Brendan put his arm around her waist and led her over to us. He grinned at me. "My cousin Karen played the part of Victoria Fear," he said. "Rachel, I guess Karen did a good job. She made you believe in ghosts, right?"

I suddenly couldn't breathe. My chest felt about to explode. Was it anger? Or embarrassment?

"I apologize, Rachel," Brendan said. "You weren't supposed to be the only one to see Karen. *Everyone* was supposed to discover her. But you ran into her room on your own."

"Sorry I scared you," Karen said to me. She shrugged. "I didn't want to do it. But Brendan can be very persuasive. He told me it was all part of a play."

I slowly unclenched my fists. "Brendan, I'm never speaking to you again," I murmured.

He made a pouty face. "It was just a game, Rachel."

I opened my mouth to tell him it was a mean trick, not a game. But there was a noise at the door. I saw Brendan's mouth drop open before I turned to the door.

Two men strode quickly into the room. They wore black sweaters and pants under khaki hunting jackets. Their faces were covered by black ski masks. They gripped hunting rifles in their right hands as they moved toward us.

I gave a cry of surprise. A tense hush fell over the room.

The masked men held their rifles in front of them in one hand, threatening us.

"Okay, everyone!" one of them boomed. "Sad news. The party's over."

29.

THE GAME CHANGES

One masked man was tall, broad-chested, and powerful-looking. He had bright blue eyes that glowed beneath the mask. His partner was shorter, a little pudgy. His safari jacket was stretched across his waist.

They both peered at us through the eye slits cut into their masks. They were dressed identically, except the blue-eyed man wore tall, dark-stained hunting boots while the other had black sneakers.

They waved their hunting rifles in front of them, showing them off, showing us we shouldn't try to make a move against them. Or a move toward the door.

My mind spinning, I dropped into the armchair beside Spider.

"That's right. Stay calm. Nobody move," Blue Eyes said. He had a hoarse, raspy voice.

"Yeah. The party is over," the pudgy one repeated.

To my surprise, Brendan suddenly began to walk

toward the two men. And as he walked, he burst out laughing.

He stepped between the two masked men. He shook Blue Eyes' hand, then turned and slapped knuckles with the other intruder. "You guys were late," he said. "I almost forgot about you."

Brendan turned to us. "These guys are part of my Panic game. One last scare. I promise this is the end of it."

He turned back to the masked men. "Take off your masks, dudes. We can all party now until the boat returns."

The men didn't budge. They eyed each other. The tall one shifted his rifle to the other hand.

"Come on, dudes. Take off the masks. Let everyone see your faces," Brendan urged.

The two men remained standing tensely. They exchanged glances again. Neither one spoke.

Brendan reached for the pudgy man's mask. The man grabbed Brendan by the front of his shirt—and gave him a hard shove that sent him stumbling backward.

Both men raised their hunting rifles, as if waiting for Brendan's next move.

"Hey—!" Brendan cried. His eyes went from one masked man to the other. "Wait. Who are you?" His voice trembled. "You're not the actors I hired. I . . . I don't know you. Who are you? What are you doing here?"

"Brendan, how stupid do you think we are?" Kenny shouted.

"Yeah. You punked us before. But you're not going to punk us again."

"Stop it, Brendan," Geena said angrily. "Enough is enough. The game is over."

Brendan kept his eyes on the two masked men. "I . . . I'm not kidding," he stammered. "Who are you guys? This . . . this isn't part of the game. I swear."

The two men shifted their weight, hunting rifles cradled in their arms.

"You're not going to scare us again," Geena insisted. "So just give us a break, Brendan."

He raised his right hand. "I *swear* this isn't a game. I really don't know who these guys are."

"You're totally sick."

"Give it up. Let's go home."

"Come on, no more games."

The tall masked man moved quickly. "You think this is a game?" he rasped.

He swung around hard—and slammed the rifle butt into Brendan's stomach.

Brendan's eyes bulged. He let out a low groan, grabbed his stomach, and fell to his knees. Still gripping his stomach, Brendan began to vomit and choke.

The gunman shifted his rifle. Then he backhanded

Brendan's cousin Karen. Gave her a vicious slap that made her drop the wig and stagger back into Eric and Spider. They held onto her, helping her catch her balance. She started to cry. The left side of her face flared bright red.

"Get up!" the gunman screamed. "Get up!" He raised the rifle over Brendan, threatening to slam the butt down on the back of his neck.

Brendan, choking, vomit staining his chin, forced himself to his feet.

"Anyone still think this is a game?" the gunman boomed.

A hush fell over the room. No one moved.

The shorter gunman moved toward us menacingly. "Shut up and stay shut up," he growled.

"You think this is a game?" his partner rasped in his hoarse voice. "This is a game you already *lost*." His blue eyes were wild beneath the black mask.

"Wh-what do you want?" Brendan stammered, wiping his chin with his sleeve. "Who are you? What do you want?"

"I thought you were supposed to be a smart guy," the chubby one snarled. "I guess you're not that smart."

"Just *tell* me," Brendan pleaded. "What are you doing here? Where are the actors I hired? What do you want?"

"You," the gunman answered.

"You . . . want me?" Brendan's voice rose in surprise. "I . . . I . . ."

The gunman gave him another hard shove. "Enough questions, idiot. We have to deal with your guests first."

I studied the taller one. Suddenly, I had this weird feeling that I knew him. Something about those bright blue eyes and his croaky voice. I struggled to remember. I'd seen him somewhere before. But *where*?

I didn't have time to think about it. The two masked men turned away from Brendan to face us. The pudgy one waved his rifle toward the door. "Let's move, everyone," he barked. "Into the hall. Now."

"You never told us about this part," Eric protested to Brendan. "You said the game would end when we came back in the room, and then everyone could party."

Brendan opened his mouth to answer but no sound came out.

The tall gunman moved quickly toward Eric. He pointed his hunting rifle at Eric's chest. "You still think this is a game, Fat Boy?"

"No. No way." Eric raised his hands in surrender and backed away.

"You'll all be safe if you keep your mouths shut," the chubby guy said. "And if you want to try to escape . . . don't even think about it."

The two men herded everyone out the door and down the hall. They pulled open a narrow door. I could see gray concrete steps leading down. Down to the basement, I guessed.

"Let's move. You'll be nice and cozy down there," the taller guy rasped. I watched him, studied his eyes, and struggled to remember where I'd seen him before.

"One at a time. And keep it quiet down there," he instructed, motioning with his rifle.

Kerry and Patti were first into the stairwell. Eric and Kenny and Morgan followed. Then Randy and Karen. No one spoke.

I could feel cold air floating up, and I inhaled the dusty, basement smell.

I moved to the doorway. "Hey—!" I cried out as the taller gunman grabbed my arm. He pulled me roughly back.

"Not you," he growled. He squeezed my arm hard and tugged me away from the others. He pulled me back to the room and shoved me toward Brendan.

"Why? Why not me?" I stammered. "Why aren't I going down in the basement with the others?"

"Just shut your mouth, or I'll shut it for good," he snarled. "Get over there with your boyfriend."

"He isn't my boyfriend," I mumbled.

The gunman hurried back out to the hall. A short while later, the hall grew silent. Then I heard a door slam. He must have locked everyone in the basement.

A few seconds later, he came striding back into our room. "Your guests can party down in the basement. If they get hungry, there are mice to eat."

Both masked men laughed at that.

I stepped up close to Brendan. He was gritting his teeth, staring hard at them. My mouth suddenly felt dry as cotton. I thought I might choke.

Do they plan to kill us now?

Brendan took a deep breath. "Okay," he said, his voice cracking. "Okay. The others are downstairs. There's no one else around. Now tell me what this is all about."

The blue-eyed man shook his head. "Haven't you figured it out, Mr. Big Shot Rich Man Fear? Seriously? You haven't figured it out? This is a kidnapping."

PART
FOUR

30.

"YOUR FATHER IS A
LOUSY CREEP"

A long sigh escaped my throat. Brendan placed a steadying hand on my shoulder. His hand was damp and ice cold. "A . . . kidnapping?" he choked out. "You're kidnapping Rachel and me?"

"Just you," Blue Eyes said. "You're Oliver Fear's kid. You're the one, buddy. Too bad your girlfriend here got involved."

"What are we going to do with her?" Chubby Guy said, swinging his rifle from one hand to the other. "She wasn't in the plan."

"No worries," his partner said. "She'll help us."

I'll help them?

I thought about the kids in the basement. I wondered what they were doing down there. Maybe they found a hidden door or a window . . . a way to escape. But even if they did . . . I knew there was no way for them to get help from town. And no way to escape the island.

"Get the rope. We have to tie them up," Blue Eyes ordered his partner. "We're going to have a long wait. We don't want you to think maybe you could make a run for it."

"There's nowhere to run," Brendan said softly. He still had his hand on my shoulder. I moved it down, squeezed his hand, and held it.

"Just tell me what this is about," Brendan said.

The two men exchanged glances. "It's about a million dollars," Blue Eyes said. They both snickered again.

"That's what your father, the great Oliver Fear, will pay to have you back safe and sound."

"So your plan—" Brendan started.

"I've been planning this *a long time*!" Blue Eyes screamed. He swung a fist in front of Brendan. "Ever since Oliver Fear ruined my life."

"Easy," his partner said, scratching the top of his head through the thick wool mask. "You don't owe the kid any explanation."

"Your father is a lousy creep!" Blue Eyes cried. He grabbed the front of Brendan's sweatshirt in both hands. "He fired me. Let me go for no good reason."

Breathing hard, he shook Brendan. Finally, he dropped his hands and took a step back.

"You worked for my father?" Brendan asked, straightening his sweatshirt.

"Accounting irregularities. That's what he said. He said I was a crook. He said he was being a nice guy not having me arrested and sent to prison. Nice guy. Ha!" He spit on the floor, just missing Brendan's sneakers.

"Okay. I made some mistakes. That's all they were. Just mistakes. People make mistakes, don't they? *Don't* they?" His voice rose. His chest was heaving up and down. I could see he was about to lose it.

"Easy, dude," his partner said softly. "You told them enough. Let's get them tied up."

But Blue Eyes wasn't finished. "I made a few mistakes. That was no reason to ruin my life. Ruin my reputation. Ruin my family. Ruin everything I'd worked hard to do."

Without warning, he slammed the rifle butt into Brendan's midsection again.

Brendan doubled over and whimpered in pain. "Please . . ." he gasped. "My ribs. I think you broke my ribs."

"I'll do worse than that," the masked man screamed. "I'll cut your head off if your father doesn't come through with my money. I'll cut your *heart* out, you punk!"

"Easy, dude," his partner repeated. "Don't lose it now. I know how you feel, but . . . we got a long time to wait here."

"Your father will pay big-time to get your butt safe and

sound off the island. We're keeping you here till he forks over a million." He turned to me. "Too bad you got involved, Rachel," he said.

"Hey!" I cried. "How do you know my name?"

He's so familiar. I know I know him. It's just . . . I'm in a panic. I'm so scared, my brain isn't working.

"Too bad for you, Rachel," he repeated. "But having you here, will just make Oliver Fear want to pay up faster." He moved the rifle. "You know. Avoid any tragedies." He stuck his face up close to mine. I could smell coffee on his breath. "We don't want any tragedies—do we?"

"N-no," I stammered. I squeezed Brendan's hand. A cold wave of panic swept down my whole body.

"We'll tie them to those chairs," Blue Eyes said, motioning to a couple of folding chairs against the wall. "Then we'll just sit and wait for our money."

Brendan narrowed his eyes at the masked man. "You already told my father you were holding us here?"

"That's not your business, kid. Want to ask another question and see how easy I can break a few more ribs?"

Brendan lowered his head. He didn't reply.

The chubby gunman leaned his gun against the wall and disappeared into the hall. Brendan and I stood in silence, avoiding each other's eyes. I found myself thinking of my sister, Beth. I don't know why she popped into my mind. I thought of how she was the scared one and I was the brave one. I didn't feel very brave now.

I raised my eyes to the rifle in the man's hand and wondered if I'd ever see Beth again. The gunman returned with two lengths of rope around one arm.

A stab of fear ran down my whole body. *What does he plan to do with the ropes?*

I poked Brendan in the shoulder and motioned to the blue-eyed one. "Does he look familiar?" I whispered.

Brendan shot me a questioning look. He shook his head no.

"Sit down in these chairs and put your hands behind you," the chubby one ordered. He dropped one of the ropes to the floor and began to uncoil the other one.

My legs were trembling so hard, I nearly missed the chair. I dropped down hard and struggled to keep my balance. My heart thudded against my chest. I'd never fainted in my life, but I thought it might happen now.

Brendan stood beside the chair next to mine. The gunman motioned him to sit down.

"Hands behind your back," he barked at me.

I clasped my hands together behind me. Even holding them tightly like that, I couldn't stop them from shaking.

The gunman bent behind me and started to wrap the thick rope around my wrists. The rope felt scratchy. He pulled it tight. Then suddenly, he stopped.

I heard a cry and raised my eyes to the open door of the room.

Someone came bursting in, running full speed.

It took a few seconds for my eyes to focus on him. And then I screamed: "Mac! No! Get away from here! Mac—don't come in! Get away! Get away! Go get help!"

31.

THE RIFLE GOES OFF

Mac didn't stop. His eyes were wild, his expression angry. He ran across the room, swinging his fists.

"No—Mac! Get away!" The scream burst from my throat. What did he think he was doing? Why didn't he listen to me? Why was he risking his life?

The chubby gunman dropped the rope and stepped away from my chair. He put his hands on his waist, ready to confront Mac.

I tugged my hands free. The rope fell to the floor behind me.

Mac roared up to the two masked men, breathing hard, his face bright red. "Give it up!" he shouted, his voice hoarse and high. "You have to give it up."

The two men narrowed their eyes at Mac, squinting from behind their masks. The tall one shifted his hunting rifle from one hand to the other. "What do you think you're doing?" he growled.

Mac sucked in some wheezing breaths. "I'm stopping you. This whole thing is crazy. You have to give it up."

Brendan and I exchanged glances. Had Mac totally lost it? What made him think he could stop these vicious thugs?

"Get out of here. I'm warning you," Blue Eyes said.

"I'm not leaving. You can't do this," Mac told him. His hands were still rolled into tight fists. His chest heaved up and down. But he seemed more angry than afraid.

"Go away," the chubby one snapped. "Go away before I lose it."

"Just turn around and walk away," his partner ordered.

"I'm serious," Mac told them. "I'm not going until you give this up."

And then without warning, Mac dove forward. He lunged at the tall masked man—and grabbed his hunting rifle with both hands. He gave a furious tug, but the man's grip held.

"Mac—no!" I screamed. Brendan and I jumped up from the folding chairs and started toward them. "No!"

We watched helplessly as Mac and the blue-eyed gunman wrestled over the rifle. The man twisted it and turned it, struggling to pull it from Mac's grasp. But Mac stubbornly held on. Grunting and groaning, he pulled, then pushed hard, trying to throw the man off-balance.

"NOOOOO!" a shrill scream exploded from my throat as the rifle went off.

The sharp *craaack* rang off the four walls.

As if in slow motion, Mac uttered a long sigh and dropped to his knees. He shut his eyes. He seemed to fold in on himself, wrapping his hands around his middle. He collapsed to the floor with one last groan and didn't move.

"Oh, no!" The tall gunman stumbled back, eyeing the still body on the floor in horror. The rifle fell from his hands and clattered to the floor in front of him.

"You shot him!" I screamed so loud, my throat ached. "You shot Mac. You murderer! You *killed* him!"

32.

A BAD IDEA

I pressed my hands to my face and stared down at Mac, so still, folded up on the floor. Brendan grabbed my arm. His mouth was open but he didn't make a sound.

The two masked men dropped down beside Mac. They leaned over him, examining him, muttering to themselves.

Brendan squeezed my arm. He motioned with his head toward the door.

I was in such a panic, it took me a few seconds to figure out what he meant. This was our chance to escape.

The two men were huddled over Mac.

Brendan and I both moved. I darted forward, grabbed the hunting rifle from the floor, swung it in front of me, and ran. Brendan was already halfway to the door.

My heart thudded like a bass drum in my chest. My legs felt shaky and weak, but I forced myself to run. Into the dimly lit hallway. I turned to follow Brendan. Our shoes pounded the worn carpet.

I glanced back as we turned a corner. The gunmen weren't coming after us yet. But I knew they would be.

I kept picturing Mac folded up on the floor. I couldn't get the image from my mind.

Why did he do such a crazy thing? Why did he think he could make them stop and give up? I couldn't think of an answer.

My brain was spinning as Brendan and I bolted around a corner. "Brendan, wait." I grabbed his shoulder. My whole body was shaking. I was gripped with panic. "If we run into the woods, they'll find us. They'll keep searching till they find us. Where can we hide? Where?"

"The elevator," Brendan said, motioning with his head. "It's down here. They'll expect us to run outside. Instead, we'll hide upstairs and wait for help to come."

Was this a bad idea? Were we making a big mistake?

I was too overcome by panic to think straight. Our shoes thudded the carpet as we ran down the long, dimly lit hall. I kept glancing back. No sign of the masked men. Yet.

Brendan pushed the button on the wall, the elevator door slid open slowly, and we squeezed inside.

I heard a shout. A man's cry far down the hall.

Did they see us?

The elevator moved so slowly, making a scraping sound as it carried us up.

Faster. Please go faster, I urged it silently, my hands squeezed into tight fists.

The tiny car bounced, a hard bump that sent Brendan and me toppling into one another. For a second, I thought it stalled. But it continued its slow, noisy climb.

Brendan and I didn't speak. The door slid open on the third floor. I followed him into the long hall. "Lots of rooms to hide in," Brendan whispered. He put a hand on my back and guided me. "That room filled with cartons. They won't see us in there."

"Wait," I said. I turned back to the elevator. It was already rumbling back down to the first floor. "If they saw us . . ."

Brendan kept his hand on my back. We both stared at the elevator door. And listened.

The air was hot and dry up here. I suddenly felt as if I was suffocating.

We both listened to the scrape of the elevator as it descended.

Were the gunmen down there? Waiting for the elevator? Waiting to come up and capture us?

I shut my eyes. *Please . . . Please . . . let them go outside. Let them think we ran into the woods to hide.*

I heard a hard bump as the elevator reached the first floor.

Brendan and I moved closer. Holding my breath, I pressed my ear against the elevator door. Listened hard.

Down below, I heard the scrape of the door sliding open. I stared at Brendan. He was frozen in place, jaw clamped tight, arms tensed at his sides.

We listened. Not breathing.

I heard the elevator door slide shut.

Silence.

Silence.

And then the hum and rumble as the little car began to climb.

"It . . . it's coming back up," I stammered. "They saw us. They're coming. We're trapped."

33.

INTO THE WOODS

Brendan squeezed my arm. His eyes darted from side to side. I could see he was thinking hard

"We're not trapped," he whispered. "Hurry."

I followed him into a dark room a few doors down the hall. I could see a pale half-moon outside the window on the far wall. The sky had turned dark. A tree branch tapped the glass.

"We're not trapped," Brendan repeated. He grabbed the window frame with both hands and pushed the window up all the way. "Look." He motioned to me.

A fat tree limb stretched under the window, almost like a ledge.

"We used to climb down to the ground on this tree all the time," Brendan said. "Just to terrify my parents." He raised one leg out the window, onto the branch. "Come on. It's easy."

He lowered himself onto the branch. "Careful. It's slippery from the rain."

Out in the hall, I heard the elevator door slide open. Heard the *thud* of heavy footsteps in the hall. Muttered voices.

I took a deep breath and dropped the rifle out the window. Then I swung myself out the window. "Whoa!" My shoes slid on the slippery, smooth limb. I lowered myself to my knees and then wrapped my legs around the limb. I leaned forward and let my hands slide around the smooth bark, following Brendan, shinnying down.

The fat limb bent and creaked under our weight. I heard a cracking sound. I screamed—and my hands slipped off the wet branch.

"Nooooo!"

I fell. Swung upside down. My head down. My hands grasping nothing but air, I gripped the branch tightly with my legs.

Hanging upside down, I reached both hands toward the branch, struggling to pull myself upright. But I couldn't reach it. My legs throbbed. I could feel the muscles giving way. I didn't know how much longer I could hold on.

"Brendan—" I gasped.

He pulled himself back up to me, swung down, and grabbed my arms. With a groan, he pulled me back up.

Gasping for breath, I swung my arms around the tree limb.

"No time to rest," he said, gazing up at the house. "Hold on. Follow me."

But the limb held us as we made our way to the trunk. I kept glancing up, expecting the masked men to poke their heads out the window above us. But . . . no sign of them.

Scrambling across the limb, it seemed like hours before we reached the fat, smooth trunk. Thank goodness it tilted at an easy angle for sliding. Wrapping my arms around it, I carefully, slowly slid down. A few seconds later, I stood beside Brendan on the grass, wiping my hands on the sides of my jeans.

The pale half-moon was still low in the night sky. Snakes of gray cloud slithered over it, making the light flicker.

"Easy, huh?" Brendan smiled. He pointed to the house. "They must be searching the rooms on the third floor for us. Come on. Let's go."

I picked up the rifle. Then we ran side by side through the tall grass, wet from the rain, toward the darkness of the trees. We didn't stop until we were hidden in the deep, inky shadow of the woods.

Brendan leaned over, hands on his knees, and struggled to slow his breathing. I had the rifle in one hand, so much heavier than I'd imagined. I pushed it into Brendan's arms. "Take it. You hold it," I said breathlessly. "I've never held a gun in my life."

Brendan nodded. He slid his hand over the butt. "My dad takes me hunting for deer sometimes." He shook his head. "I'm a terrible shot, but . . ." His voice trailed off.

Owls hooted up ahead. The tree limbs shifted in a gust of cold October wind, cracking and sighing.

"Where are we going?" I asked, glancing tensely into the deep shadows.

"To the dock," Brendan said. "The long way. Through the woods. So they don't catch us."

I nodded. I listened for the two men. I didn't hear anything. High above us, the owls seemed to be having a conversation, hooting at each other.

"The two masked men must have come in a boat," Brendan said. "If they anchored it at the dock, we can take it to town."

"Mac said he had a canoe," I told Brendan. "When I saw him in the hall. Before . . . before . . ."

"Maybe we can find it," Brendan said. "It will be big enough for us to escape."

The word *escape* rang in my ears.

The horror tonight was supposed to be a game. Brendan had it all planned. But it turned real and ugly. Deadly. Mac was lying dead on the floor. And Brendan and I were witnesses.

The gunmen would come after us out here, I knew.

Kidnapping had turned to murder. They couldn't just keep us here. They had to silence us.

"We'll be okay," Brendan whispered. "I promise." He swung his arms around me. The rifle bumped my back. He pulled me close. I pressed my cheek against his.

"I . . . I've never been so frightened," I confessed.

He held me tighter. "Stay close, Rachel. I know these woods better than anyone. I spent my whole childhood playing here. They'll never be able to get to the shore as fast as we can."

We both jumped back when we heard the voices.

Men's voices, accompanied by the scrape and brush of feet on the leafy floor of the woods.

"Do we really have to kill them?" one of them said.

I froze.

I didn't hear the murmured answer.

Brendan's eyes went wide. He heard it, too. He raised a finger to his lips. Then he pointed through a row of fat shrubs to a narrow path that cut between them. He motioned for me to follow.

We both took off, heads bowed low. We tried to run in silence. But it was impossible in the thick carpet of crunchy, crackling leaves and twigs.

I signaled to Brendan to wait. "Maybe we should stop and hide and let them pass by," I whispered.

He shook his head. "Our only hope is to get to the

dock." He waved the rifle in front of him, and we took off running again.

The path twisted and turned, almost impossible to see in the total blackness. Every once in a while, a shaft of pale silvery moonlight would light our way.

Over the hoarse sound of my breathing, I could hear the men behind us. They were murmuring to each other, their footsteps rapid. Closer.

A low branch scratched my face. I gasped. Forced myself not to cry out. My cheek was cut. I could feel a warm trickle of blood on my skin.

Brendan took my arm and guided me off the narrow dirt path. Stepping high over weeds and fallen tree limbs, we made our way blindly into the trees. Brendan signaled with the hunting rifle, and we turned again. My shoes splashed in a deep puddle of muddy water.

I gasped at a stab of pain in my side. I pressed a hand against it. The sharp ache made it hard to breathe. I stopped running. Bent over. Waited . . . waited for the pain to fade.

Finally, I started to feel better. I stood up straight. Two fat tree trunks rose in front of me, black against the purple-black sky. I could barely see. The trees stood as if blocking my path. Something scampered over my feet and darted through the crackling, dead leaves.

I gazed around, forcing my eyes to focus. "Brendan? Hey—Brendan?" I called in a hoarse whisper.

No answer.

I squinted into the darkness. I couldn't see him.

"Brendan? Where are you?"

I listened for his footsteps. I could hear only the creaking of the tree limbs over my head and the rapid sighs of my breathing.

"Brendan? Hey—Brendan?"

Why didn't he answer?

34.

LOST AND ALONE

I froze. I held my breath. I listened for any sound, any sign of him. A night bird trilled loudly in a tree behind me. It sounded like laughter. Human laughter.

I spun around. No one there.

A chill shook my body. I hugged myself, gazing beyond the fat trunks of the twin trees in front of me. I tried to shut away my breathless panic and try to decide which way to go. If only we had stayed on the path. I could have followed it one way or the other. Maybe I would have come out at the dock and found Mac's canoe. Maybe I could have paddled it back to Shadyside and found help.

But the tall trees circled me, as if holding me inside, holding me in a prison cell. Gazing up, I couldn't see the moon, so I couldn't even begin to figure out what direction I was facing.

The strange bird trill burst out again, making me jump.

Shrill laughter from high above me. I took a deep, shuddering breath and started to walk.

If I can keep going straight in one direction, I'll come out either at the house or the water.

I didn't go far. I stumbled over a rock and landed in a nest of thorny vines. They seemed to tighten around my ankles, thorns digging into my skin. I tried to pluck them away carefully, but they kept scratching my hands.

When I finally freed myself, I stood up, my fingers throbbing with pain. I heard voices. Up ahead. Squinting hard, I couldn't see anyone. But I heard a harsh shout. Then a high-pitched cry.

The *crack* of gunshots made me gasp and drop to my knees. I felt the cold, wet dirt seep into my jeans. The sharp *cracks* bounced around the woods, first in front of me, then behind, the sound ringing off the trees.

When the sound abruptly faded, I stayed on my knees, hugging myself, listening hard, afraid to breathe. My first thought: *Did they shoot Brendan?* And then: *Are they going to hunt me down now? Am I really going to die here in these woods? Stalked and killed like an animal?*

I forced myself to stay silent. I knew they were nearby. Maybe only a few yards away.

They shot Brendan. They shot Brendan.

Please . . . please let it not be true.

I heard the scrape and scratch of footsteps. The sound of a twig breaking under a shoe. To my left. I drew in a deep breath and held it. My throat tightened. I felt like I was about to choke.

And then I heard a man's voice. I recognized it—the voice of the tall gunman.

"We got the boy," he said. "Now let's get the girl."

35.

THE DEATH PIT

The black trees appeared to spin around me, like a fast merry-go-round. The ground tilted up, then down. Suddenly dizzy, I shut my eyes and tried to think.

They shot Brendan. They're forgetting their kidnapping plans. They killed Mac. Now they just want to kill us, the only witnesses.

A picture of my dad and my uncle in their hunting outfits tore into my mind. I saw them cleaning their rifles, preparing to go out on the hunting day they enjoyed together once a year. Hunting for deer.

Tracking down prey.

Now *I* was the prey. These two masked men with their hunting rifles tensed, their shoes crackling over the leaves, so near I could hear every leaf crack. At least, in my terrified condition, so tense and alert, I *thought* I could hear every leaf crack.

So close. Close enough to reach out and touch?

For some reason, my friend Amy broke into my pan-
icked thoughts. *Amy, why didn't I listen to you? You begged me
not to go to this party. You warned me not to get mixed up with
Brendan and the Fear family.*

Why didn't I listen to her?

Because of my crush on Brendan?

I didn't listen to Amy. And I didn't listen to Mac.

And now . . . now . . . here I was . . . more frightened
than I'd ever been. Frightened for my life.

I opened my eyes. The trees had stopped whirling
around me and the ground had settled beneath my knees.
Slowly, silently, I stood up.

I heard the men cursing in low voices. I didn't hear
Brendan. Their footsteps were rapid and loud. They were
heading in the opposite direction, away from me.

Yes.

I waited. Staring in their direction, I stood shivering,
and waited. Waited till I could no longer hear them. Then
stood still a few minutes more. To make sure.

And when I was certain they were not playing a trick.
When I knew they weren't lying in wait, setting a trap, I
took off in the other direction. I forced my legs to move,
kicking leaves and twigs and small branches out of my
way, using my arms to brush open a path between shrubs
and clumps of tall weeds.

I didn't know where I'd come out. I just wanted to run
as far as I could from the two gunmen. I didn't have a

plan. I couldn't think straight at all. I was running through a nightmare, a nightmare of black shadows. And all I could see in my mind was Mac crumpled on the floor in that room . . . Brendan's body, sprawled stiff and still on the ground. Brendan's body and my dad and uncle in their L.L.Bean hunting jackets and tall hunting boots, waving their rifles, and the deer running . . . trotting full speed through the trees . . . the deer running so frightened . . . so frightened like me.

Then—more terror. The ground gave way. It just vanished. And I fell into a hole, my hands flying above my head, my feet kicking wildly.

Black walls rose up on all sides, and I dropped hard and fast. I landed on my feet, but my legs collapsed and I crumpled onto the bottom. I expected dirt or mud. But something hard cracked and slid beneath me.

I struggled to catch my breath. I gazed up at the sky and saw a rectangle of gray light high above me. A pit. I had fallen into a deep pit, the dirt walls rising high above my head.

My knees throbbed with pain from the fall. A wave of panic shot down my body. Did I break my legs? Could I stand?

Slowly, I pulled myself up. No. No. My knees pulsed with pain.

I can't walk. I'll never get out of here.

I took a deep breath and forced myself upright. Bent

my knees until the pain started to fade. Stood hard on one leg, then the other. Everything hurt and I had a few scratches, but I seemed to be okay.

My shoe kicked something hard on the pit floor. Had I landed on rocks?

I bent to see more clearly. I picked up the strangely shaped rock I had just kicked.

I raised it close to my face to see it in the darkness. No. Oh, no. I wasn't holding a rock. I held a skull . . . a human skull.

I tossed it to the pit floor. It rattled against something hard and rolled to the wall. I bent down. Pale moonlight suddenly cast a sick green light over the pit, and the bones came into focus. Long bones. Short ones. A rib cage. No. Two rib cages. Another skull grinning up at me with its deep black eye holes and all its teeth.

Bones. A thick jumble of skulls and bones.

I was standing in some kind of human burial pit.

I tried to hold it in—but how could I?

I opened my mouth in a long, hoarse shriek of horror.

36.

NO ESCAPE

The scream ended in a shuddering moan. The pale shaft of moonlight made the bones glow a dull yellow-green. I tried to look away from the tilted skulls grinning up at me.

As if welcoming me. Grinning to see a new victim of the pit, a new resident. *Join us . . . Join us—forever. . . .*

"Ohhhh." I moaned again as the putrid odor of death floated over me. I started to gag. The smell was thick and sour and . . . and . . . I held my breath and waited for my stomach to stop heaving.

Who were these poor people who ended up together at the bottom of this deep hole in a stinking jumble of bones? Were these the Fear family servants who were killed in that bizarre hunting party? Could that story possibly be true? Could anyone be so cruel to shoot their servants for a sport and dump their bodies in a pit in the woods?

I trembled in horror and tried not to think of the people

whose remains I was standing on. Tried to keep my eyes on the small rectangle of moonlight above me.

Brendan. Where are you, Brendan? Are you okay?

Brendan was a Fear. Did he know about this burial pit? Did he know that the horrifying stories about his ancestors were *true*?

I didn't want to think about that. I just wanted to know that Brendan was safe and alive. I just wanted him to be alive.

I'd heard the rifle shots and the words of the gunmen:

"We got the boy. Now let's get the girl."

I leaned my back against the pit wall and listened. Had the two gunmen heard my scream when I discovered the bones? I could hear only the rush of the wind above me. So far, they hadn't found me. But they had to be nearby.

I took a few steps. The bones crunched under my shoes. A skull rolled toward the dirt wall. The moonlight dimmed for a few seconds, then returned.

I knew I had to find a way out of the pit. The walls rose up at least three or four feet above my head.

I dug my hands into the soft dirt wall. Could I climb up the side?

I suddenly pictured the rock-climbing wall at the Shadyside Mall. Beth was the timid one in the family—except when it came to that climbing wall. She loved it. She was so sure-footed and confident and strong. I never could keep up with her.

But could I do it now? Could I pretend I was on the rock-climbing wall and pull myself up?

I had to try.

I gazed up at the smooth dirt.

No way. No way. No way the soft mud would hold my weight. The mud would crumble off, and I'd slide back down onto the floor of bones.

Bones.

Yes. Bones.

I suddenly knew I had no choice. There was only one way out of this disgusting, putrid hole.

I bent over and grabbed a leg bone and shoved it against the dirt wall. I swept three or four more bones into my arms and piled them on top of the first one.

The bones were cracked and caked with mud. Many of the skulls were crawling with insects. Tiny white worms climbed in and out of the nostril holes.

My stomach started to lurch again. I tried to hold my breath to keep the smell from making me sick. But I *had* to breathe. I knew the smell would linger with me, stay on my clothes and my skin.

I tried not to think about that. I had a mission now. A plan. A plan to pile the bones up against the side of the pit. To use them to climb to the top and escape.

I lifted two rib cages from the floor and pushed them on top of the pile. I tossed a skull to the side and grabbed a few more leg bones. I needed to pile them three or four feet high. That would be enough for me to climb up and grab the ground at the top of the pit. Once up there, I was sure I could pull myself out.

I decided my bone pile was high enough. I stepped onto the bones at the bottom of the pile, reached up, grabbed bones above my shoulders with both hands . . . leaned forward and tugged myself up.

"Whoa! Nooooo!" The bones made a heavy clattering sound as they slid out from under me. I toppled back to the pit floor, landing facedown between two skulls. I lay there, sprawled on my stomach, breathing hard for a few seconds. Sharp bones dug into my stomach.

You can do this, Rachel.

If those men find you down here . . . they'll kill you and leave you in this pit.

My skeleton will join the others.

The thought made my breath catch in my throat.

I forced myself to breathe. Then I began shoving bones back against the wall. I tossed them and rolled them and piled them up again. Working feverishly, I jammed rib bones on top of leg bones, tucking them in, trying to make my bone ladder more sturdy.

After I'd piled the bones three or four feet high, I began scooping up mud in both hands, spreading mud over the bones, like cement. I patted the mud tight in the bones, smoothed the bones with it, scooped more mud, hoping it might hold the bones together beneath me.

Then I took a deep, shuddering breath and again began the sickening climb.

You can do this, Rachel.

Fat black bugs scuttled over my hands. I brushed them away as I grabbed and climbed, digging my shoes into the bones beneath me.

The bones trembled beneath me. I heard a clattering sound. The bone ladder began to slide apart.

My head pressed against the dirt wall, I made a wild grab for the ground at the top. My hands slid back. I started to fall.

I dug my fingers into the dirt. "Yesss!" I hoisted myself up, my legs frantically bicycling against the pit wall. Hoisted myself . . . pulled . . . and hurtled like a raging animal out of the disgusting pit and onto the solid ground above it.

I hugged the ground, breathing so hard I thought my chest would explode. I knew I couldn't stay there. I knew I didn't have much time. The kidnappers had to be nearby.

I forced myself to my knees, brushing fat black bugs off my arms, off my clothes. I stood up, my legs shaky, my shoes bringing up clumps of mud.

Silence all around. Even the wind had stopped. Where was Brendan? Where were the two gunmen who were hunting me?

I'd lost all sense of direction. The moon had disappeared behind clouds again. I couldn't tell which way led to the house and which to the water. But, my head spinning, my throat aching, I started to move anyway.

I walked away from the pit, eager to leave it far behind. Into the trees, brushing away tall weeds and saplings as I moved. My legs felt too shaky to run. But I kept up a steady pace. Walked until I found a dirt path that wound through the tall trees, black against an even blacker sky.

I walked with all my senses alert, listening for sounds of my pursuers, my eyes scanning the darkness for any movement. The dirt crunched under my shoes. Despite the cold air, I kept mopping sweat off my forehead with the back of one hand.

My heart started to pound when a broad stretch of gray opened before me. I realized I had come to the end of the trees. Squinting hard, I could see a wide patch of tall grass, waving first one direction, then the other in the swirling wind.

The wind gusts grew stronger. The air suddenly felt heavy and wet.

I stepped away from the forest of trees, onto the sweeping grassland. And almost cried out for joy when I saw the water. Yes. The lake. Low, purple waves lapping at the grassy shore, such a soft and soothing sound.

The lake. I'd reached the lake. Mac's canoe. The boat the gunmen came over on. They had to be at the dock.

I can escape. I can get back to town and get help for Brendan—and for the other kids.

Shielding my eyes with one hand, I gazed down the shore and saw the dock jutting out into the lake. Yes. I'd reached the dock, stretching over the water like a huge dark insect. Squinting hard, the cold wind blowing against my burning face, I stared at it.

And then I let out a low moan.

The dock stood empty.

No canoe.

No boat.

No escape.

37.

WET

I stared at the dock, as if willing a boat to appear. The tall grass tilted around me in the steady rush of swirling wind. The only other sound was the gentle splash of the dark waves against the dock pilings.

I thought I heard something. I sucked in a mouthful of air. I spun around. Away from the water. Squinted into the trees. No. No one there.

You're alone here, Rachel. What are you going to do next?

A strange feeling of calmness had fallen over me. I realized that I could take only so much fear, feel only so much panic. And then a weird feeling of numbness made me let out a long, weary sigh.

I started to breathe normally. I tucked my hands into my pockets. I stopped trembling. I turned back to the dock.

So okay. I couldn't escape the island by boat. A new plan was definitely needed.

What are you going to do, Rachel?

My brain was spinning. I could almost hear the gears going around. I knew I didn't have many choices. I could wait here near the dock, just in case the servants' boat was really returning as Brendan said it would.

I could go back to the house. Maybe I could set the kids in the basement free. Then we'd outnumber the gunmen and . . .

No. That was stupid. And dangerous.

What other choices did I have? I could hide in the woods . . .

The strange calm I felt quickly began to dissolve. I thought about Brendan. Had they killed him? Did they really plan to kill me?

The *whoosh whoosh whoosh* of footsteps over the tall grass came so fast, I didn't have time to think.

They were coming. Nowhere to hide here. The tall grass wouldn't hide me. No way to slip into the shadows of the dock.

The running footsteps grew louder.

My chest felt about to explode. My head throbbed with panic. I glanced all around.

I had to hide—or else I was dead.

I lurched forward and stepped into the water. I had my eyes on the log pilings that held up the dock. If I could slip behind them . . .

So cold! Oh, so cold. The shock of the cold water made it hard to move.

I can't do this. My teeth are chattering already.

My shoes felt so heavy on the sandy lake floor. I leaned forward—strained against the cold—and forced myself to move. In seconds, the frozen water was up to my knees. My whole body shivered.

"Oh. Oh. Oh." The icy cold water made me moan out loud.

I reached the pilings. Wrapped my arms around one of the tall logs. Swung myself behind it.

The low waves bobbed, rising to my shoulders. I held onto the dark logs. Pressed myself behind them.

I'm out of sight here. But I'm going to freeze to death in a minute or two. Or drown.

I held my breath, trying to stop my body from shuddering. Water filled my shoes, soaked my clothing, holding me down. A tall wave sent water sweeping up to my chin.

Water splashed into my throat. Thick and icy cold. I started to choke. I clung to the wet, slippery log. Struggling to breathe, I gagged, then spit out water and shut my eyes against another wave.

Were the two men on the shore? Had they seen me hide here?

I couldn't hear them over the roar and splash of the waves against the pilings.

Holding tightly to the log, I peered out. Turned myself so I could see the shore.

Water ran down my eyes. I tried to blink it away.

I'm going to die here. I'm going to freeze to death.

"Rachel—" A hoarse voice called.

Huh?

They've found me. They've got me.

I turned. I leaned my head and peeked out from behind the pilings. And gasped in surprise.

"Mac? You're alive? Mac? Is it really you?"

38.

HELP

His hair was wind-blown, wild about his head. His eyes were wide, intense.

He nodded. "I'm alive."

He moved to the water's edge. I reached out my hands. I let him pull me from the lake.

My clothes were soaked. Water ran down my face. I couldn't stop shivering. But I stared at him in disbelief. "I-I thought . . ." I stammered.

"You thought I was shot?" He shook his head. "No. I wasn't hit." He tried to brush his hair down with both hands.

"I . . . saw you go down," I stammered.

"I wasn't shot. I faked it," he said. "I wanted to give you and Brendan a chance to escape. The bullet hit the wall. It didn't even come close to me."

I didn't know what to say. Seeing Mac was like seeing a ghost. More like seeing Patti, Kerry, and Eric alive again.

Only Mac wasn't playing a game. And the rifle the tall gunman fired was real.

He tugged off his leather jacket and wrapped it around my trembling shoulders.

"Mac . . . How did you escape? How did you find me?"

"They both ran out," he said, his eyes still locked on mine. "They went after you and Brendan. I waited till they were gone. Then I took off. I figured . . ." His voice trailed off.

"You were so brave in there," I said. "You came running at them. I thought . . . I thought you were crazy. But . . ."

Mac finally lifted his gaze. He turned and glanced behind him. "We have to hurry, Rachel. Follow me."

"Follow you? Where?"

He motioned up the shore. Above us, the moon reappeared. Mac's eyes glinted like silver in the sudden light. "Come on," he whispered. "There's no time. I have a canoe, Rachel."

He started to trot through the tall grass, following the shoreline. "I hid it on the other side. Away from the dock. Hurry."

I hesitated. *Should I follow him? What about Brendan?*

If I got back to town, I could get the Shadyside police. I could rescue Brendan and the kids in the basement

Mac motioned to me impatiently. "Come on. Move. Let's go. I'll get you off this island."

"Okay. Thank you." I spoke the words in a trembling whisper. *Was I really getting out of this nightmare alive?*

Leaning into the wind, I followed Mac across the grass. Our shadows were long under the moonlight, like fingers stretching out in front of us. We followed the curve of the island. Slender trees poked along the waterline, leaning forward as if trying to escape the island, too.

Another sharp curve found us back in the woods. Silvery moonlight darted in and out, making it all seem unreal, making the trees appear to pop in and out.

"Mac—where are we going?" I cried. "It took me so long to find my way out of the trees. And now—"

"My canoe is around the next curve, Rachel," he replied. He waited for me to catch up with him. Then he put a hand around my waist and guided me through the maze of trees and underbrush.

I couldn't wait. I wanted to see that canoe. I wanted to be on the water, crossing the choppy, black waters to safety.

"Around this way," he said, tightening his arm around me. He guided me over a fallen tree limb and through a narrow opening between low evergreen shrubs.

"But we're heading *away* from the water. Aren't we—"

I stopped when I saw the men in the small clearing past the shrubs. The two masked gunmen. And Brendan. Yes. Brendan was with them. One of the gunmen held Brendan's arms behind him. The other stood waiting for Mac and me, rifle poised at his side. "Welcome back," he said.

A trap. Mac led me into a trap.

I spun hard and faced him, my anger bursting out of me. "How *could* you? Why? Why, Mac? Why did you do this to me?"

39.

BETRAYED

Mac still had his arm around my waist. I spun away from him, glaring at him furiously.

He took a step back. "I'm sorry," he said softly. "I had to bring you to them. I didn't have a choice. I had to."

"Had to?" I cried. "Why?"

"He's my dad, Rachel. I knew you recognized him. I had no choice. I couldn't let you get away."

"Your dad?"

Of course. That's why the blue-eyed gunman seemed so familiar.

In my panic, my brain wasn't functioning. *Of course it was Mac's dad.*

Dwight Garland.

Garland tugged the ski mask off his head and tossed it to the ground. His shaved head glistened with sweat. His steel blue eyes narrowed at me. He'd never been very friendly. I always thought he didn't like me. But now I saw more than anger on his face. I saw a hardness, an expression that went beyond cold.

"Thanks, Mac," he said in a flat voice. "We couldn't let Rachel get away—could we?"

I stared from Mac to his dad.

No wonder Mac knew so much about what was going down here. No wonder he tried to stop me from coming to the party. He knew what his father had planned.

"I really did try to stop him," Mac said to me. "I really did try to take away the rifle. But . . . once I figured out that you recognized him, I had to protect him. I had to bring you back to him."

"Shut up, Mac!" Garland snarled at his son. "Just shut up. I mean it."

Mac had it wrong. I didn't recognize his father. But, what did that matter now?

Still masked, the other gunman kept his tight grip on Brendan. Brendan had his head lowered, his shoulders slumped. But now he raised his eyes to me. Even at a distance, I could see the terror on his face.

"We're in trouble here, Rachel," Brendan said. "We're in major trouble."

"Shut up!" the masked gunman snarled. He jerked Brendan hard. He turned to Dwight Garland. "What are we going to do with these two? They know who you are. We have to kill them. Don't you see? We can't let them—"

"I haven't decided," Garland snapped.

"Maybe we can make it look like they killed each other," his partner said.

"You can't kill them, Dad," Mac chimed in. "No way. It's bad enough you kidnapped them. But you . . . you're not a murderer. You can't . . ."

"I told you—shut up!" Garland snapped. "I never wanted you involved in this. I told you to stay away from the island. If you had just listened to me for once in your life. . . ."

"Let us go," Brendan said. "Let us go, and I promise— we won't tell anyone about this. We'll pretend it never happened. Really." Brendan was breathing hard. "And I'll tell my dad to pay you. I will. I'll get you the money. I promise."

Garland laughed. "You sound like a bad movie."

"It isn't funny," his partner said. "We can still collect the ransom, Dwight. But if we don't kill them, we'll be caught for sure."

Garland didn't reply. He was studying Mac. Mac had his fists balled tightly at his sides. He was breathing hard, his chest heaving up and down.

"Mac, I want you to go home now," he said finally. He motioned with his head. "Get in your canoe and get out of here."

"But, Dad—"

Garland raised a hand to silence him. "No arguments. I want you home. I don't want you here if . . . if bad things happen." He stepped beside his partner. "Go, Mac. Now."

Mac had his jaw set tight. He curled and uncurled his fists. He glanced at me, his face tight with anger. Or fear. I couldn't tell what he was thinking.

I didn't care what he was thinking or feeling. I could feel my own anger boiling up inside me.

I didn't think. I didn't hesitate. I knew this might be my last chance to act.

With a furious cry, I dove forward and grabbed Mac with both hands. I squeezed my hands around his shoulders— and *heaved*. I heaved him hard, with all my anger, all my strength.

I was startled by how light he felt and how little resistance he gave. He went sailing, stumbling backward and toppled into his father and the other kidnapper.

Cursing loudly, both men went down, tumbling onto each other. The rifle bounced out of Garland's hand and slid over the dirt.

"Brendan—*move!*" I screamed. I knew we had only seconds till they were back on their feet.

I spun away. I hurtled into the trees. I heard their angry shouts behind me. I heard Mac scream, "Put the gun down!" I heard curses and then the *thud* of shoes on the dirt.

Was Brendan right behind me? Did he get away?

Without slowing down, I turned back. "Brendan?" No. No, he wasn't there. He didn't escape them. "I'll get help, Brendan," I murmured to myself, a promise I hoped I'd be able to keep.

I ducked under a low tree limb, covered in dark moss. A tangle of prickly brambles scraped my ankles, but I didn't slow down. I kicked them away as I ran. Yellow-green moonlight cast eerie shadows all around. I tried to ignore them, but each shadow made me think the two gunmen were running beside me.

I'm running for my life. If they catch me, they'll kill me.

A voice from behind me—*close* behind me—called my name. "Rachel. Rachel—stop."

Mac's dad. Did he see me? His running footsteps seemed to be coming from my right. I turned. I couldn't see him. He was coming after me by himself. His partner must have stayed back at the small clearing, holding Brendan.

I stopped running. I lowered myself behind a tall, slender pine shrub. I struggled to slow my wheezing breaths. I listened.

"Rachel—you can't get away." Garland's voice sounded farther away. Back in the trees. "Listen to me. I'm not going to kill you. I swear. I'm not a killer, Rachel. Do you believe me?"

He stopped running. I knew he was searching for me in the trees. Searching and listening.

I held my breath. I tried to squeeze myself smaller to hide behind the slender shrub.

"Rachel? I know you're here," Garland called, more tense, his voice tight and shrill, ringing off the bare trees. "I'm not going to hurt you, Rachel. We're just going to keep you and the Fear boy here till the money arrives from his father. Then you'll never see us again."

A long silence. My nose itched. I squeezed it hard. I knew a sneeze would be my doom.

"Do you hear me?" Garland called. "Can you hear what I'm saying?"

Good. He doesn't see me. And he doesn't know how close I am.

"Do you believe me? Come out, Rachel. I'm not going to hurt you."

I heard a splash behind me. A soft wash of water. Silently, I turned my head from the shrub. Through a clump of slender trees, I could see the dark outline of the water. The lake. I didn't realize I was so near the shore.

I held my breath and didn't move. I heard Garland mutter something to himself. A few more low curses. Then I heard the crack of leaves and the soft *thud* of his shoes on the ground. I listened hard, so hard my ears were ringing.

He was moving away from me.

"I'm going to find you," he called. "You can't escape."

I waited, listening to the scrape of his fading footsteps. Waited. A very long wait, it seemed. An eternity.

Then when I felt certain he wasn't nearby, I rose to my feet. My back ached from hunching so long behind the shrub. I tried to stretch the pain away. Then I took off, heart pounding, walking carefully, hurrying to the water.

I stood at the soft grass on the shore. Water lapped over my already-soaked shoes. Moonlight sent ripples of gold on the low waves.

I nearly cried with happiness when I saw the canoe. It was perched down the grassy shore, paddles tilted over its sides. A beam of yellow moonlight played over it like a spotlight.

A canoe. Mac's canoe.

I took a few cautious steps toward it. I'd never paddled a canoe. But I knew it wouldn't be hard. Beth and I had gone kayaking with our cousin on a lake last summer. That was easy and fun. A canoe couldn't be much harder.

I took a deep breath and trotted toward it. The ground became soft, and my shoes splashed up mud as I ran. I planned my moves as I ran. *Push the canoe into the water. Climb in and grab a paddle.* I was a few feet from the canoe when the voice rang out sharply behind me.

"Stop right there, Rachel."

I turned to see Dwight Garland, his bald head glowing in the moonlight, hunting rifle poised, raised to his shoulder.

"N-no—" I stammered.

"Just stop right there. Step away from the canoe." He

249

motioned with the rifle. "Don't just stand there," he snarled. "Move away!"

"No," I repeated. My throat felt so tight, my voice barely escaped. "No. I'm going. You won't shoot me."

"Step away," Garland insisted, taking a step toward me. He slid the rifle onto his shoulder. The barrel was pointed at me. "Don't test me, Rachel. I don't want to hurt you. Step away."

"No!" The word burst from my mouth again. I moved to the back of the canoe and lowered myself to shove it off the grass and into the water.

"Step away!" Garland screamed. "I warned you!" And then he fired the rifle. One shot. Deafening.

I shrieked and my hands flailed up in the air.

Another shot.

He lowered the rifle barrel and fired again. Again.

I gasped and my body collapsed to the muddy ground.

40.

"NO ONE WILL BLAME ME"

On my knees in the mud, I clamped my eyes shut and waited for the crushing pain.

Silence now. The silence of death.

The pain didn't come. Was I already unconscious?

No. I opened my eyes to see Garland standing over me, rifle lowered at his side.

"Huh?" I whipped around in confusion. It took me a few seconds to see what he had done. He shot the canoe full of holes. Made sure it would never float.

I let out a long sigh. My shoulders slumped. I wasn't dead. But maybe I soon would be. Garland's eyes were crazy, staring at me with too much intensity, like lasers he wanted to burn right through me.

"I asked you nicely," he murmured. He swept a hand over his bald head. "Why didn't you listen to me?"

"Why should I?" I snapped. "Were you telling the truth? I don't think so."

He grabbed me roughly by my ponytail and tugged me to my feet. The legs of my jeans were soaked and caked with dirt, but I didn't bother to brush them off. "Were you telling the truth?" I repeated. "Is Brendan okay? Is he? Are you going to kill Brendan? Are you going to kill me?"

He spit on the ground. "Brendan's okay. But it's gotten complicated, hasn't it? Very complicated." He jerked me forward. I could feel his anger. "Let's go. It's cold out here."

We walked in silence through the woods to the house. He kept two or three steps behind me. I guess, in case I decided to make a run for it.

If I did try to escape, would he shoot me?

I could hear him muttering to himself. I realized the tension was getting to him. His eyes were wild. He was cursing to himself now, obviously agitated.

He's losing it. Totally losing control. This can't be good for Brendan and me. If he goes completely crazy . . .

The thought tightened my throat. I felt as if I couldn't breathe.

The dirt path curved and then began to rise up the sloping hill to Brendan's house. The rain clouds had floated away. Dotted with tiny white stars, the night sky brightened. The bare tree limbs overhead gleamed dully, casting long shadows across the path.

I saw another curve up ahead, through two fat tree

trunks. My heart began to *thud* as I decided to attempt an escape. Maybe I could whip around one of those trees and disappear into the woods before Garland could raise his rifle.

Maybe he wouldn't shoot.

Maybe.

I didn't think about what I'd do *after* I got away from him. I just knew my life depended on escaping. As we reached the sharp curve, my skin started to tingle. My whole body began to quiver. I took a deep breath and held it.

I tensed my leg muscles, preparing to run. The wide tree trunks, bark draped with moss, loomed ahead me.

I'll run on the count of three. I'll spin, push off from the trunk, dive into the darkness behind it.

Sounded like a plan.

One . . . two . . .

But, whoa. I didn't follow the plan. My body didn't do what my brain had decided.

With a hoarse cry that sounded more animal than human, I swung around. My shout startled Garland. He stopped. His mouth dropped open.

I roared again and leaped forward. Without thinking, I shot out both hands and grabbed the barrel of the hunting rifle. I swung it left, then right. He struggled to keep his grip on the stock.

But I jerked it easily away from him.

The rifle dropped from my hands and hit the dirt. We both dove for it.

I got there first. I wrapped my hand around the stock and raised it in front of me.

A look of fear crossed Garland's face. His blue eyes went wide as he climbed to his feet and took a few steps back.

I raised the rifle to my shoulder and aimed the barrel at him. I'd never fired a rifle in my life. But he didn't know that.

He raised both hands, as if in surrender. But he said, "Give it back, Rachel. Give it to me."

I didn't reply. I motioned with the rifle for him to keep his distance.

Slowly, he stretched out his hands, reaching for the gun. "You're not going to use that. You know you're not. Hand it back to me, Rachel. Don't make me fight you for it."

I stared at him, trying not to let him see my trembling hands.

"Don't make me fight you for it. You'll regret it."

"I . . . I know how to use this," I said. "Keep back. I'm warning you."

He hesitated for a moment, his eyes on the rifle. Then he dove for it.

I pulled the trigger. The gun exploded against me, a powerful jolt that made me stagger back.

Garland made a rough choking noise and reached for his throat. Bright blood spurted over his hand.

I fired again and watched a dark stain spread quickly over the chest of his shirt.

He groaned and slumped to his knees. Blood gushed like a fountain from his neck and his chest. His body twitched crazily, and then he went still. He toppled onto his back and lay in a puddle of dark blood. His blue eyes stared glassily up at the brightening sky. He didn't move.

"Yes!" I pumped my fist in the air. "Yes! One down and one to go. Now I'll kill his buddy. Why not? No one will blame me."

41.

"YOU SPOILED CREEP"

Two fat tree trunks stood like guardians at a curve in the dirt path. Past the trees, the path sloped up sharply, leading to the house.

"You're awful quiet," Garland said. "What are you thinking about?"

I was tempted to tell him that I'd just imagined shooting him twice and killing him. How would that go over?

Well, Mr. Garland. I just pictured myself grabbing the rifle and blasting holes in your neck and your chest and watching you bleed to death.

He probably wouldn't appreciate that. And since he was already muttering and cursing crazily to himself, sweat pouring down his bald head despite the cold night, I decided to keep my thoughts to myself.

"Nothing much," I said.

The huge house came into view beyond the front lawn, the swaying grass gray in the moonlight.

"Mac messed this up," Garland grumbled. "He wasn't supposed to be here. He wasn't supposed to get involved. The jerk. The stupid jerk."

We walked on. I didn't say anything. I knew he was talking to himself.

"Mac told us there was gonna be a party here," he continued. "That's when we realized how easy it would be to kidnap the Fear punk on this island." He shook his head. "Easy. It was supposed to be easy. But then Mac said you recognized me. He said you'd identify me. Blow the whole deal."

"Mac tried to warn me last week," I said. The words just spilled out.

Garland exploded in an angry roar. "He *what*? Mac told you about this? He told you what we were planning?"

"No," I said quickly. "No. He didn't tell me anything. He—"

"Why didn't he just put it on Facebook?" Garland shouted. "Tell the whole world? He *told* you we were coming here?"

"No. No way." I turned to plead with him. "Mac didn't tell me anything. He just said he didn't want me to come to this party. He—"

"Shut up!" Garland boomed. He swung the rifle barrel at me. "Shut up! Shut up! I have to think." He rubbed his bald head. "I have to figure this out. My son . . . my idiot son . . . what was he *thinking*?"

I walked in silence. Mac's father was acting more and more deranged. He talked to himself all the way back to the house. I couldn't hear what he was saying, but it sounded like he was having a big argument with himself.

We found Brendan and the other gunman in the ballroom. Brendan sat glumly on a folding chair near the fireplace. He had his hands tied behind his back.

The pudgy gunman stood a few feet away, still masked. His rifle leaned against the corner of the back wall. The fire had died. The room smelled of wood smoke. The air felt cold against my hot cheeks.

I turned and saw Mac, hunched in a chair against the far wall. He was all folded-in on himself as if he was trying to disappear. He glanced up when his father and I stepped into the room. Then he lowered his eyes and turned away.

"That's right. Don't look at me," Garland yelled to his son. "Don't look at me. I'm warning you."

"But, Dad. Give me a break. I brought her to you, didn't I? *Didn't* I? I didn't want to, but I helped you."

"Don't look at me. Last warning."

Mac sighed and turned away.

Garland pushed me onto a chair beside Brendan. His partner tied my hands behind my back. I whispered to Brendan, "You okay?"

He shrugged, avoiding my eyes. "You okay?"

"No," I said. "How could I be okay?"

"Shut up! Shut up!" Garland screamed.

His partner's eyes went wide in surprise. "Hey, what are we doing? What's the word here, chief?"

Garland was red-faced, sweating. "I didn't want Mac involved. But that idiot warned the girl. He probably called the police, too."

"I did not!" Mac exclaimed angrily.

The masked guy stepped up to Garland and blocked his path. "You said this would be easy. Easy money, you said. Kids locked in the basement. Oliver Fear pays, and we are out of here. You promised me, Dwight. You didn't say anything about . . . about . . ." He motioned to Brendan and me.

"Shut up. I mean it. Shut up. Let me think," Garland said, rubbing sweat off his head.

"There's nothing to think about," his partner insisted, spitting the words in Garland's face. "They know who you are. We're already caught. We have to drop it and get out of here. Or else . . ."

He pulled a knife from his pocket. He unfolded the blade and swung it in front of him.

A chill of horror shook my body.

"We won't tell anyone," Brendan said. "I told you before. I promise. We won't tell anyone. Just let us all go. We won't say a word. My father will pay and he'll help you get away. The money means nothing to him."

"You spoiled creep," Garland muttered with a scowl.

"Let's just kill him," the masked one said. The knife blade gleamed in his hand. He stepped in front of Brendan. "I really want to kill him, Dwight."

"No—please!" I screamed.

Brendan didn't plead. Instead, he glared up at him. "You don't have the guts," he said through gritted teeth. "You can't kill me if you want the money. Even someone as stupid as you knows that."

The gunman growled and lowered the knife to Brendan's throat. "If I'm so stupid, how come *you* are the one who's going to die?"

"No—wait, Sal," Garland interrupted. "The punk is right. We need him alive."

"Thanks, Dwight. You told him my name. Nice move." He tugged the mask off his head and heaved it to the floor. He had curly red hair and green eyes and a crooked beak of a nose. His face was drenched with sweat from the mask.

"We need him alive, Sal," Garland insisted.

"But we don't need the whining girlfriend," Sal said.

A horrified moan escaped my throat. I strained at the ropes, but it was useless. I couldn't move.

"Wait—" Garland insisted.

But Sal didn't wait. He swung around to me, his green eyes wild.

"Wait!" Garland screamed. "Listen to me, Sal. Don't!"

Sal ignored him. He pressed the knife blade against my throat.

I shut my eyes.

Oh, please. Oh, please—no.

I heard the rush of air as the knife came slashing down.

"Stop! Don't!" Brendan wailed.

"Too late," Sal rasped. "Too late."

42.

CUT

I felt a stab of pain. At the back of my head. A hard tug.

I opened my mouth to scream, but no sound came out.

Struggling to breathe, I opened my eyes.

Sal had turned to Garland. He gripped the knife in his right hand. In his left fist, he held my ponytail.

My ponytail. My ponytail. I don't believe it. He cut off my ponytail.

He tossed back his head and roared with laughter. Then he flung the ponytail into my lap. "You two still feeling so brave?"

I stared at the ponytail in my lap and shuddered.

These men were both crazy. Were Brendan and I going to get out of here alive?

"You've had your joke, Sal," Garland said. "Now put the knife away and give me some time to think."

"I've had it with your thinking," Sal shouted at Garland. "Your thinking hasn't exactly worked out, man. Maybe *I* should do the thinking from now on."

He took two steps toward Garland, holding the knife in front of him.

Garland raised his hunting rifle. "Back away, Sal. I mean it."

Sal gestured with the knife. He took another step toward Garland. "You blew this, man. You're finished. And thanks to your brilliant plan, I'm going down with you."

"Put the knife down, Sal. Back away. I don't need you. I'm going to get the money. With or without you."

Sal stood his ground. "We have to kill these two. If we want to get away . . ."

"*I'll* decide what to do with them. Not you. Not you, Sal. Now back away. I'm going to count to three."

Sal kept the knife poised. He didn't step back.

Garland counted. "One . . . two . . ." He had the rifle pointed at Sal's chest.

"Dad—no!"

Mac suddenly came to life. He leaped off his chair and came running at his father.

Sal tossed the knife to the floor. He dove forward and grabbed Garland's hunting rifle with both hands. Garland twisted it, tugging hard, trying to wrest it away from his partner.

I tensed every muscle. Was the gun going to go off like before? Was someone about to die?

"Dad! Stop! Stop it!" Mac stood helplessly, watching the two men wrestle for the weapon.

Brendan and I were helpless, our hands tied to the back of the chair.

Garland cursed and screamed as Sal continued to battle him for control of the gun. "I'll kill you! I'll kill you *all*!" Garland wailed.

I gasped as the door to the room burst open. Brendan and I both screamed as two, dark-uniformed police officers came running toward us, pistols raised.

"Drop your weapons!" one of them screamed. "You're under arrest!"

With a powerful jerk, Garland pulled the hunting rifle free of Sal's grasp. He swung it onto his shoulder and aimed it at the officers.

"Drop your weapon!" both cops shouted in unison.

Garland hesitated. A long moment. Then he angrily tossed the rifle to the floor, sending it skidding to the officers' feet. Garland slowly raised his hands above his head. Sal stood frozen beside him, red-faced, his mouth open in shock.

Mac stepped over to us and untied Brendan and me. I stood up. My ponytail fell to the floor at my feet.

I shuddered. *What a close call.*

I gripped the back of the chair, and waited for my legs to stop trembling and my heart to stop fluttering. But Brendan appeared totally calm. He stepped toward the two

264

officers, shaking his head. "Just in time," he murmured. "You guys are just in time."

The two cops exchanged glances. They kept their guns drawn. They were both young and tall and thin. One of them had a narrow, tanned face and a black mustache. The other one was boyish looking. He could pass for a teenager.

The mustached cop stepped up to Brendan. "What's going on here?"

"It's a kidnapping," Brendan replied, motioning to Dwight and Sal. "For real. They came here to kidnap me. Take them to your boat."

"They were going to kill us!" I cried. "If you had come a few minutes later . . ."

The cops' eyes widened in surprise.

"They weren't serious," Mac chimed in. "It wasn't real. My dad didn't mean it. Really. They—"

"Shut up, Mac," his dad snapped. "You're not helping anyone. I told you to stay home."

The boyish cop turned his gaze to Mac. "You know him? He's your father?"

Mac nodded. He didn't reply.

"Your father came here to kidnap these two people?"

Mac had a bitter scowl on his face. "Just Brendan."

"Shut up!" Garland screamed at Mac. "Shut up! Shut up! Are you going to stand there and confess before they even arrest us?"

"You are under arrest," the young-looking cop said.

"My other guests are locked in the basement," Brendan said. "I'll get them out. You need to take these three to your police station."

"Right," Mustache replied. He waved his pistol at Dwight and Sal.

"Contact my father," Brendan said. "Oliver Fear. Tell him to send the boat to pick everyone up. Rachel and I will come tell you the whole story after everyone is rescued."

The cops both nodded. "Get going," the boyish one told Dwight, Sal, and Mac. "We will read you your rights on the way back to Shadyside." They pulled handcuffs off their belts and handcuffed Dwight and Sal.

My hands still gripped the back of the chair. My chest felt as if it was filled with butterflies. As I watched the two cops collect the hunting rifles and lead the two men and Mac out of the ballroom, I wondered if I would ever feel normal again.

Would I see that rifle pointed at me every time I closed my eyes? Is it possible to get over the horror of someone aiming a weapon at you and threatening to kill you?

The door closed hard behind them. Brendan and I were left alone in the vast ballroom.

He stood watching the door, as if expecting them to burst back in. When he finally turned to me, he had a strange expression on his face. I couldn't read it. Was he actually *smiling*?

He walked up to me and led me gently away from the folding chair. He wrapped his arms around me and pulled me into a hug. His cheek felt blazing hot against mine. I couldn't stop trembling, even in his tight embrace.

Finally, I stepped back. "Brendan," I said, his warmth still on my cheek, "those policemen . . . How did they know to come here?"

"They didn't," he said. His eyes crinkled as he smiled.

"Huh? Did you call them?"

"No. The phones don't work here, remember?" he said.

"But then . . . How did they know we were in trouble?"

"They didn't know it, Rachel." A wide grin spread over his face. "It was part of my game."

"What?" I screamed. "The whole kidnapping thing—?"

He shook his head. "No, that was real. Dwight and Sal were really here to kidnap me. And they might have killed us. That wasn't a fake."

"But the two cops?"

"They were part of my Panic game. They were supposed to burst in and arrest all the guests. But they were late, I guess because of the rainstorm. . . ."

My brain was spinning. My head felt about to explode. "Brendan, please. I'm totally confused. Those two cops . . . ?"

"They're not real cops," Brendan said, still grinning. "They're actors I hired." He laughed. "They looked more surprised than the kidnappers. I could see them shaking. Couldn't you?"

"No," I said. "No. I believed them. I believed they were real cops. I thought maybe they were just new."

Brendan shook his head. "Their guns weren't even real. We got them at a theater prop store. But I guess they were real enough for Garland and his partner."

"That's insane!" I cried. "The whole thing. Just insane! You're crazy, Brendan. You really are." Impulsively, I threw my arms around him. I pressed my mouth to his.

He let go of me and started to the door. "We have to let the others out. They're going to be very confused."

"I hope . . . everyone is okay," I said, following him out to the hall.

He turned to me. "Now I have one major problem."

I narrowed my eyes at him. "What problem?"

"What am I going to do for my birthday *next* year?"

43.

MORE HORROR?

A week later, I was back waitressing at Lefty's after school, trying to pretend that everything in my life was back to normal. I say *pretend* because it wasn't exactly true. I was having vivid nightmares every night in which I was being chased by someone who wanted to kill me.

And the short walk home after work now filled me with anxiety. Every leaf that blew against my ankle made me jump. Every moving shadow made me cringe with sudden fear.

"It'll take time," Mom said. "But it's all over, Rachel. Just keep telling yourself it's all over."

Well, I guess it *was* all over for me. And for Brendan, too. We spent hours in the police station explaining what had happened—to *real* police officers this time.

Dwight Garland and his partner, Sal, were charged with kidnapping and assault.

And as for Mac . . . Well, the situation was pretty

messed up. He was being charged as an accessory to his dad's crime. But it hadn't been decided whether Mac's case should be tried in a juvenile court or adult court.

So, things weren't exactly normal even though I pretended they were. I didn't even take a day off. I went back to school on Monday and back to Lefty's as if nothing had happened.

I was mopping around a table after two little kids spilled most of their dinner on the floor when Amy walked into the restaurant. She wore a red hoodie over faded jeans. She gave me a wave and sat down in the first booth.

Amy had been a wonderful friend all week. She had been so understanding and kind when I described what happened on Fear Island. And she never once said, "I told you so. I told you not to go."

She even said she liked my new short haircut.

It was a quiet night at Lefty's. The restaurant was nearly empty. Most kids from school were home studying for midterms. I walked over to Amy and dropped across from her in the booth. "Hi. What's up?"

"Did you hear about Mac?" Her eyes were wide with excitement.

"Good news or bad?" I said.

"Good news for him. The police dropped all charges. They said he wasn't an accomplice. Because he tried to stop his father."

"Wow. That's good," I said. "Did you hear? Is he coming back to school?"

"No. He and his mom are moving. Again."

"Wow," I murmured. I didn't know what else to say.

Amy brushed her hair off her forehead. "Have you seen Brendan?"

"We're going out next week," I said.

"So you two are seeing each other?"

"Kind of," I said. "We went through so much. I guess it made us kinda close."

Amy nodded. "You mean like brother and sister, or what?"

I didn't answer. "He's so weird," I said. "He confessed to me he was sorry he scared everyone so badly at his birthday party. But, know what Eric told me? Eric told me Brendan is working on a scary new game for his next party."

Amy rolled her eyes. "Another scary game? You're kidding."

"That's what Eric said."

"I warned you about him, Rachel. Seriously. I warned you about getting involved with someone in the Fear family. They're all totally weird. I mean it."

I shook my head. "You're wrong, Amy. Brendan isn't *that* weird. Besides, we're taking it a day at a time."

That was a lie. I still had a crush on Brendan. If only he

could give up the games. The disaster at his party hadn't cured him at all.

"I just stopped by to say hi," Amy said, climbing to her feet. "I'll be up all night studying for the Chem test. Call me later?"

"For sure," I said. I heard the kitchen bell. I stood up and started to cross the restaurant. I glanced back in time to see Amy walk out the front door—and someone else enter.

At first, I didn't recognize her. She was too unexpected and too out-of-place. Impossible. But after a long moment of confusion, I realized I was staring at my sister, Beth.

I recognized her smile first. I thought, *Beth can't be here.* But, there she was. She had a navy poncho over a short black skirt, and black fur-topped boots nearly up to her knees. Her dark hair was different. It had blonde highlights in the front.

Lefty hit the kitchen bell again, but I was racing down the aisle to hug my sister. We wrapped our arms around each other and held each other tight, as if she'd been gone for years instead of only a few months. She smelled of cinnamon. Her cheek was cold from the air outside.

"Beth—I-I don't believe it!" I stammered. "When did you get home? What are you doing here?"

She practically had to peel me off her. "I came to see you," she said. "You look okay."

"Yeah. I'm fine. But . . . how—?"

"I heard you had a bad time, Rachel. Mom called me. She told me all about it. She said I didn't have to come home, but I wanted to."

"I'm so glad. I'm . . . stunned. Really. I . . . I missed you so much, Beth."

She shook her head. "I'm sorry. I haven't been good at keeping in touch. I didn't know freshman year would be so challenging. I mean . . . it's so different."

She looked just like Mom when she frowned like that.

"No worries," I said, squeezing her hand. "How long can you stay?"

"Just till Sunday night. I can't miss my Monday classes. But we'll have plenty of time to talk. I want to hear everything, Rachel. I mean, you can tell me anything you like about what happened at that party."

"Well . . ." I'd been dying to talk to her about it. But now I felt reluctant. I guess because it was pretty much over.

"I know," Beth said, her eyes flashing. "We'll have our good old weekend, do everything we did back in the day. We'll hang out at the mall Saturday afternoon and laugh at all the weird people, and try on a million things we won't buy, and run into everyone we know. Then we'll call out for two pepperoni pizzas, and be total couch potatoes, and watch the *worst* horror movies all night on Netflix."

My mouth dropped open. I grabbed Beth by the shoulders. "Horror movies? *Horror* movies? I don't think so."

Beth and I had an awesome weekend. We spent so much time talking, laughing, and having fun, I didn't get to unpack my bag until after she left. That's when I discovered something missing.

In all the horror and excitement, and my eagerness to escape Fear Island, I'd left my tangerine jacket behind. The jacket I treasured because my aunt in New York had sent it. I remembered where I left it, in the ballroom when we came in from the rain. I called Brendan. "Did anyone find a jacket? The clean-up people? Did they bring back an orangey jacket?"

"No. No jacket," he said. "It's probably still where you left it, Rachel."

"Can we go get it?" I asked. "I really need it. I mean, is the house open?"

Brendan arranged for a motorboat and pilot to take us to Fear Island on Saturday afternoon. It was a dark day with heavy storm clouds low in the sky, a lot like the day of the party. A steady, cold wind pushed the waves high around us as we roared toward the dock.

Seeing it as we approached made me shiver. *Too many bad memories on this island.*

It started to rain just as we reached the house. A jagged bolt of lightning crackled over the roof.

Brendan fumbled with the keys and finally unlocked the front door. "Go find your jacket," he said. "I'll be right there. I want to check something in the garage."

I pushed back the hood of my parka and stepped into the front entryway. The air was cold in the house. There were no lights. I glanced down the long hall to the big ballroom where the party had been held. The wood floors gleamed in the gray light from the hall windows.

The house was silent except for my footsteps as I made my way to the ballroom. I pulled open the doors and stepped inside. The room was bare. No furniture. No jacket.

Maybe I left it upstairs in that bedroom, I told myself. I hurried back down the hall and took the stairway to the second floor. I stopped at the landing and gazed down the hall. Clean and silent and empty.

I turned and started to the first bedroom. The bedroom had been cleaned. The beds were made. The dresser top empty. No jacket. No sign of my jacket.

I checked the closet. I got down on the floor and looked under the bed.

No. Someone must have found it and . . . Maybe they hung it in the coatroom downstairs.

Stepping into the hall, I heard a sound. A scrape. And soft *thud.*

"Brendan? Is that you?" My voice rang out down the empty hallway.

No reply.

A rectangle of light slanted out from a bedroom door-way down the hall. I heard more noises. Was someone else here? Brendan said the house was empty.

I strode down the hall, slid the bedroom door open, and stepped inside.

I gasped when I saw the long table at the far end of the room. It was covered with animal parts. Squirrel legs. A bushy tail. A cat torso. A stuffed owl perched on a block of wood.

Oh, noooo.

Then I saw the woman behind the table. She had her back to me. I could only see her long, scraggly white hair flowing down her back. Flowing over . . . my jacket.

She was wearing my tangerine jacket.

"Excuse me!" I called out. "Hello?"

She didn't move at first. Then slowly . . . very slowly, she turned around.

And my mouth dropped open in a silent cry.

She had no face. The long white hair framed a grinning skull. A skull perched over my jacket. Her sunken eyes remained on me as she picked up a small knife—and plunged it into a fat squirrel belly.

I finally found my voice and uttered a shrill cry.

I heard running footsteps. From the hall.

I spun around. Brendan burst through the doorway. "Rachel? What's wrong?"

I turned and pointed. "S-She—" I stammered.

He squinted at me.

I gaped at the front of the room. No one there. And no dead animals. No animal parts. The table stood completely bare—except for my tangerine jacket, balled up on one corner.

"You found it. There's your jacket," Brendan said. "What is your problem?"

Trembling, I grabbed his arm. "Brendan, this room. T-This house . . ." I stammered. "All those old stories. The house . . . it really is haunted. . . . It—"

Brendan laughed. He squeezed my hand. "Come on, Rachel," he said. "You don't believe those crazy stories—*do* you?"